A BDSM Extravaganza: 8 Explicit Stories of Erotic Dominance and Submission

By Alexandra Noir

Table of Contents

Aimee sat in her office, idly looking out of the window. Her thumb ran along the bottom of her ring finger. It felt strange to feel her bare flesh rather than the hard golden ring that had been sitting on her finger for the past nine years. She smirked when she thought about her wedding day and the vows she had made to Aaron, her ex-husband. They had promised themselves to each other for eternity, but that promise had been broken. She turned to her computer monitor and checked the figures for last month's views, and she sighed. Nothing she did seemed to bring more traffic to the website. She hated how the world had changed. No longer could she just print a magazine and send it to stores, now she had to control a website and have content constantly uploaded. It was a strain on her, and she honestly wondered how much more she could take, but she didn't know what else she could have done with her life. It was almost as though she was trapped, for her youth had slipped away without her noticing and suddenly she was approaching forty with no family, no husband, and the constant fear that she wasn't going to accomplish anything else with her life.

Her phone rang, interrupting her thoughts. She groaned inwardly when she saw who was calling.

"Hi Greg," she said, trying to sound happier than she felt.

"Aimee, how's it going?"

"Oh, it's alright."

"I was just looking over the figures for last month's views and I think we need to have a conversation."

"I was just looking over them myself. I was about to call you actually," she lied, but Greg always liked it when people took initiative.

"Yes, well, do you have any comments?"

"Just that I'll do everything I can to make them improve. I've got some good ideas for content and I'm sure we'll see an upturn."

"Well, I'd like you to send me an email with all your ideas. I've already taken a big hit on physical sales because of the interneti, and I don't want to keep throwing money at something that isn't working. If things keeping going the way they are, I'm going to have to downsize again."

"That won't be necessary. I promise I'll figure something out," Aimee cast her gaze out at the small office and the skeleton crew of the magazine. If there were any more losses she would basically be doing everything herself.

"Make sure you do. If I'm not making money, then—"

"You don't have to say any more, Greg. I'll take care of it."

"I'll be waiting for that email to hear your ideas. Make sure they're good ones," he said tersely. The call ended and Aimee leaned forward, placing her head in her hands. It felt as though everything was plummeting and now she had to worry not only about her job, but about the jobs of everyone else in the office. Aimee's head throbbed, and she wished she could just escape. It felt as though she had to take care of everything; there was no respite, no way of letting go.

She opened a window to a new email and started writing to Greg with all these wonderful ideas she was supposed to

have, but the problem was she didn't have any. She was
burnt out creatively, and anything she thought of seemed
trite and bland. She looked towards a picture hanging on
the wall of her office of her accepting an award. She'd been
younger then and filled with energy, wanting to change the
world with her words. But over time, the passion had
became a job and her energy had greatly diminished. Now,
she did what she did for a paycheck and nothing more, and
she hated that about herself. She wasn't sure when things
had changed; it had been more of a gradual decline than an
abrupt transformation. She was certain that her marriage to
Aaron had been a part of it.

Closing her eyes, her mind returned to the days of her
marriage. First, she thought about the early days when she
had been in the full flush of love and lust for the charming,
intelligent, sweet man that seemed so different from all the
others. He had won her over with his sense of humor and
his compassion, but that initial flurry of love had faded
over time. Aaron had always expressed his admiration and
attraction for Aimee's confident, authoritative side, which
she had liked at first because there had been a lot of men
who had been intimidated by her. Not so Aaron, who was
proud and delighted with her for being so successful in her
career, but she had noticed how he always deferred to her
in everything. She had wanted a partner in life, but
throughout their marriage, she realized that it was she who
was making all the decisions, she who was propelling them
forward, and it got to a point where she was exhausted.

Aaron promised he would try to change, but he never did.
Perhaps, he was incapable of changing. Aimee didn't hate
him for that. It was just a shame that they couldn't be who
each other needed in the end. She wanted someone

stronger, someone she could defer to in the end. She was tired of being in charge all the time, but it seemed as though there was no escape from this fate as she had to summon all the reserves of her strength to pull this magazine back from the brink.

She began to type out a few ideas, hoping that if her fingers flew across the keyboard she might suddenly be struck with inspiration. Instead, she grew angrier with herself and wished that she could pluck ideas from thin air again like she had been able to when she was younger. The nature of creativity intrigued her because it had always been elusive, and she had always been afraid that one day she would lose what made her special. Maybe, the day had come and she was just too stubborn to realize it. Maybe, it had been ground down and eroded by the tattered marriage. Maybe it had disappeared forever.

One thing Aimee didn't want to do was resort to cheap click-bait tactics that were so prevalent on other websites. She'd seen enough vapid articles online for a lifetime, and she hated how so many sites only seemed to want to drive traffic to their website without providing content of any quality. The most galling thing of all was that it seemed to work. Getting plaudits for quality content was all well and good, but at the end of the day the only thing that mattered to Greg was the bottom line. If she couldn't improve the performance, he would find somebody else who could, or he'd just pull the plug on the magazine altogether.

These were supposed to be the best years of her life; the years when she sat back and enjoyed all the hard work she'd put in during her youth. Instead, it seemed as though the climb was never-ending, like there was no end of obstacles in her way. Something was missing. She just wasn't sure what 'it' was, or how to go about finding it.

***

Aimee had been staring at a blank screen for what seemed like hours. She had typed out the beginnings of about fifty ideas for new features and articles, but had deleted them all because she was sure that they had been done elsewhere, and had been done better. She lamented the loss of the magic spark of her youth, the burning flame inside her that seemed to be able to pull out a shard of inspiration whenever she needed one. She grew tired and her eyes ached. All she wanted was to slip into a hot bath with a glass of wine and let the aches and pains of life drift away.

Instead, there was a knock on her door. She looked up to see Jack standing there, so tall and young and handsome. She envied whichever girl had captured his attention, and then chastised herself for being a naughty older woman. His blue eyes sparkled and his tousled hair was messy—in a confident way—a way that suggested he didn't care what anybody else thought of him. He had an easy smile and carried himself well. He was also a good writer and a diligent worker, and Aimee knew he'd go far in the industry.

"How are you doing?" he asked, closing the door behind him. He carried in his hand a few sheets of paper.

"I'm okay," she said, gesturing for him to have a seat, but he remained standing for the moment. She looked up at him, which she did most of the time because he was over six feet tall, and she was a modest 5'5. "I've just been trying to think of some new features to dig us out of this hole we've gotten ourselves into. I just don't understand it.

I'm proud of the work we've been doing, but people just don't seem to be biting."

"It'll come in time. I think part of the problem is the marketing. It's all well and good writing this content, but if nobody knows our website exists, it's going to be a problem. I've been working on the social media side of things, but it's going to take a big marketing push to get eyeballs on our site."

"And like everything else, that's going to take a lot of money; money that I'm not sure Greg is going to spend." Aimee could already hear him say how he had put too much of his own money into the running costs of the website already. "It annoys me how you always need money to make money."

"That's just our beautiful world, but look, the reason I came in here is because I wanted to show you something. I wrote an article that's…well, it's more personal and a little riskier than what we usually showcase on the site. I wanted to show you first because, if you don't approve of it, then it can stop here. I'd appreciate some discretion because I don't want what's in this article to get out to anyone else in the office. I thought that, if we went ahead with this, we could say it comes from an outside contributor."

Aimee's curiosity was piqued. So far, Jack's work had been reliable and informative, if lacking in a little creative flourish, so she was intrigued by his proposal. She held out her hand, eager to see what he had written. Jack, however, held onto the paper. He pursed his lips and hesitated for a moment.

"I would just like to say that I'm offering this to you in a professional manner. I think that there are certain things in the world that need to be addressed, and the things I talk about in this article…I hope they don't affect my role at this company. I know that you are an open-minded person, and I hope that you read this article with that spirit." He nodded and then folded the sheets of paper, placing them onto her desk, before rising and leaving her office.

Aimee arched an eyebrow and picked up the article. She was about to open it when the phone rang again. It was Greg, nagging her about the email.

"I'm sorry I haven't gotten anything to you yet, Greg. I've been brainstorming ideas with the writers down here, and we've got some exciting ideas. I've also just gotten something very interesting from…an anonymous source. I have a feeling it might change the course of the magazine. I'm going to collate the ideas and send them to you first thing in the morning."

Greg sounded annoyed. He grumbled and told her that he expected to see something exceptional. Aimee assured him he would. She hoped that what Jack had provided to her would live up to her claims of excellence. After having endured another tense conversation with Greg, Aimee knew that she couldn't stay in the office for any longer without going crazy. It was starting to feel more like a prison, so she rose from her desk and strode out, taking Jack's article with her.

***

The light had faded quickly, something that Aimee didn't always realize when she was in her office because the windows were tinted and seemed dark and murky all the time. The day blended into the night as though time was just melting away, as though the days of her life were trickling down like grains of sand in an hourglass. Before too long, she would be down to the last dregs.

Returning home, she grabbed some leftovers from the previous night's meal and drew herself a bath, lighting candles all around her apartment to illuminate her world in a soft glow. The scent of vanilla and lavender filled the air around her, and warm steam rose from the bath. Soft, foamy bubbles cascaded atop the water. She poured herself a big glass of wine to help her relax. It only took one sip for a gentle haze to ripple across her mind and for warm tingles to reach down to the tips of her toes.

She slipped off her work clothes, breathing a sigh of relief as she stepped into the bath. Warm water seeped over her exposed flesh as she sank down. The bubbles swarmed around the sensual curves of her supple, feminine body, covering her in relaxing warmth. She moaned with delight as the water came up to her chin. The bath was deep and the wine went down well, teasing away the tension that had been building up in her mind. The soft glow of the candles provided a naturally relaxing atmosphere, helping her to slip into a tranquil state of mind.

When the glass was half-empty, she reached over and grabbed the article that Jack had written. Her fingers were dry, so she didn't have to worry about staining the pages. She was ready to see why Jack had been so coy about the contents of the article. The truth revealed itself as soon as she saw the title of the article.

Confessions of a Dominant: My Journey Through the World of BDSM

Aimee's breath caught in her throat and she felt her heart thump in her chest. Even though Jack had told her it would be personal she had never expected anything like this, and she was tempted to stop reading altogether. But no, he wanted her to read it. He wanted to share this deeply personal story, and Aimee wanted to read it.

By looking at me, most people would never know of my secret desires, but I want to share them with you because I think there's too much of a taboo around certain lifestyles that consensual adults enjoy. I know there are plenty of people out there who might be struggling to find meaning and fulfillment in their relationships, who might wonder why they don't feel satisfied with the person they love. I'm here to tell you that it's okay; you just might have certain desires that you don't even know about yet.

That's what happened to me.

My relationships always failed, and I wasn't sure why until I became aware of the BDSM lifestyle. As soon as I began to research it more deeply, I realized what I had been missing in life and why I hadn't been happy. It also became clear that, once I delved into this wonderland, I wouldn't be able to go back, nor would I want to because I've discovered so much about myself and about my relationships with people. I'm more confident, more determined, and I have a better sense of what I want from my relationships. It's made me more discerning when it comes to romantic partners, and I've never been more at ease with myself.

I hope that this article can help you learn a little more about yourself, and maybe even shed light on a secret desire you've harbored without even knowing it.

Once Aimee started reading she found herself unable to stop. Jack had gone on to write about the nature of BDSM itself, about the exchange in power between the Dominant and the Submissive, about the blurring of pain and pleasure and the sweet delirium that came with the trusting bond between two consenting adults. The more he described, the more she found herself excited by the thought of giving up control, of being used and ordered around, of pleasing someone who knew what they wanted and what they needed from her.

As Jack described some of his kinks Aimee found herself holding the paper with one hand. Her other hand slipped below the water's surface to find the hidden parts of her body, then slid down her flesh to the hot part in between her thighs. The bubbles hid her rampant desire and sweat began to trickle down her temples. She became acutely aware of the heat emanating from the candles and her breathing became rapid. Her hand moved, and she groaned loudly. Waves began to lap against the side of the bath and some water even splashed over the edge, not that she cared. Her mind was alive with thoughts of Jack standing over her, so powerful and young, teaching her how to be a good submissive, taking care of her, leading her into a wondrous place of passion and lust. She wouldn't have to think about anything. She wouldn't have to make any decisions. She could just be…

Her eyes opened in small fluttering blinks to gaze at the words on the page, reading his experiences over and over again, imagining his mellifluous voice reading the article to her, whispering in her ear, his arms wrapped around her as he lay underneath her. Breath rushed out of her as she imagined him touching her, and as she slipped her fingers inside her, she believed them to be his fingers. Aimee became a slut for his touch.

***

She pulled herself out of the bath, her body still thrumming with passion. Her mind dripped with desire and her mouth hung open. She pulled the plug and the water drained away, the bubbles spiraling down the bath. The papers had been flung onto the floor, as she'd had to grip the edge of the bathtub with all her might as an intense orgasm hit. Now, her heart was still beating rapidly, as she was yet to calm down. She couldn't remember the last time, if ever, she had experienced something as strong as that climax. It had all been from Jack's words. Her mind had been opened to this world, and she found it alluring.

She wrapped a soft towel around her and patted away the droplets of water that lingered on her body, her mind rampant with ideas, but did she have the courage to approach Jack about this? She was his boss, after all. It was never a good idea to mix business with pleasure, but he certainly knew what he was talking about. The more she thought about it, the more she was certain it was what she needed. She couldn't imagine how overwhelming the pleasure would be if she was intimate with Jack in person. Just the idea of it had left her reeling.

Doubt lingered in her mind, as she crawled into bed, but she knew one thing for certain; she needed change in her life. There had always been something missing, and this might well be it.

Her throat ran dry as she thought of delving into this world, though, because she knew there would be no turning back. At least with Jack, it would be with someone she knew; if he wanted to teach her, that is. She worried that she was too old to learn new tricks. He was so experienced. He probably had no end of potential partners. But he was right in saying that she never would have guessed he had this side to him. He seemed so gentle and polite, to think of him being dominant and powerful—reducing a woman to a toy, ready to be used and abused and pushed to her limits—was almost unfathomable. The more she thought about it, the more her desire to learn grew.

***

The following day, she returned to the office and was not entirely sure how the day was going to go. She felt refreshed, though, and had the energy to type out a few ideas, outlining Jack's proposal as well. Jack's piece was on-the-edge content which the website needed, but it wasn't tawdry or salacious and handled the material in a respectable and responsible manner. Greg okayed the idea. Now, Aimee was left with the problem of how to actually approach Jack without creating any awkwardness between them.

She called him into her office during the middle of the morning. Now, when she saw him, she couldn't see anything other than a dominant man. Her gaze drifted down his body, and she lingered on his hands, thinking about how he could control her. She swallowed the lump in her throat and then she gestured for Jack to take a seat. She tried to retain a professional demeanor even though her blood swam with desire.

"I take it you read my article?" he asked.

"I did, and I was impressed. I liked how you tackled the subject matter with discretion and respect. I also liked how you wrote it as an educational piece, tackling the misconceptions surrounding the lifestyle."

"That's a relief," Jack smiled and clasped his hands together. "I hoped that was the way it came across, but I wasn't sure. It's difficult when you're writing something so personal. I wanted to make sure that I didn't get it all jumbled up."

"Not at all. It was all very concise and I think there's a lot of potential here. Did you have any ideas about how to make this into a regular feature?"

"I did actually. I thought I could talk about different aspects of the lifestyle and write about some of my real life experiences, maintain my privacy and the privacy of my partners, of course. I also thought it might be a good way to engage interaction from our readers. I'm sure there are a lot of people out there who are interested in this but don't have the courage or knowledge to experience it properly. And people might be too ashamed to speak of these desires, so it might help to bring those walls down as well. I don't expect to change the world, but I've encountered plenty of people who are confused about what they want. If I can offer them some clarity, then I'll be extremely happy."

As he spoke, Aimee felt herself drifting away and thinking about him giving her orders, about him tearing her body apart, and now that she was in close proximity to him, she felt a fevered and fervent desire bubbling up inside. She wondered if he could sense her yearning, her craving.

"Get working on your second article. I think these are all great ideas, and I'll figure out a way to make them work. We'll run this one first and see what kind of reception it gets, but I can't see it being anything but positive."

"It's going to be controversial. A lot of people still have misguided opinions about the lifestyle," he warned.

"Oh, I know," she replied with a cocky smile, "but that will only help to drive traffic to the site. It'll certainly get people talking." He grinned back and nodded at her sharply before he rose, ready to leave and get back to work. Aimee knew she couldn't let this chance slip so she called him back.

"What's up?" he asked. Aimee froze, almost afraid to ask him what she needed to ask him. The last thing she wanted was to come across as a desperate, lonely woman, clinging to a slender thread of hope. But in that moment, she wasn't his boss; she was just a woman hoping that she would be worthy of an experienced dominant.

"When I was reading your article…this lifestyle, I…I became intrigued. It's almost like, in places, you were talking about me, and I want…I wondered if you could teach me."

Jack clenched his jaw. His gaze seemed to bore into Aimee, as though he was peering directly into her soul. Aimee dipped her head away. Tingles rippled over her body. The mere thought that he would even consider taking her as his submissive set her heart on fire.

He glanced away, towards the rest of the office, before turning back to her.

"Are you sure you want this? It's not for everyone, and it might interfere with our dynamic here."

"I've thought about that, and I do want it." She rose from behind her desk and walked towards him, standing in front of him, looking up at him. "I want you to teach me everything you know about this lifestyle. Is it possible to keep it separate from our working lives?"

"It's possible, yes. We'll have to set up boundaries, limits, and rules. The most important thing is that you're comfortable with everything. Do you know what you want to explore?"

"I just want to feel powerless. I want to give up control and surrender myself to you. I don't want to be a boss. I don't want to be in charge. Show me what it's like."

Jack stepped closer to her and lowered his voice. "You mean to say *please* show me what it's like, *sir*." Aimee's heart shuddered and she corrected herself, already feeling the first flush of submission. "I'll come to your house tonight after work. Wear something that will please me. Your training will begin immediately."

He briskly walked out of her office, leaving Aimee reeling. She staggered back and placed her hands against the desk, steadying herself, taking in deep breaths to try and hold her composure. She watched Jack walk back out to the office knowing that he was going to train her, and none of the others were any the wiser. This gave the affair an illicit, secretive thrill, only adding to the allure and excitement that Aimee felt.

***

Jack had given her the task of wearing an outfit that would please him. She opened her closet and pulled out an array of clothes, eventually settling on some white, lacy lingerie, a short skirt, and a low cut top that showed everything she had to offer. She wanted to expose as much flesh as possible, but still leave something for Jack to discover. She poured a couple of glasses of wine and then awaited his arrival, her nerves rising with every passing moment.

Eventually, she heard a knock at the door. Jack was standing there, carrying an authority that just wasn't present every day at work. She welcomed him in. He gave her a look over and nodded with approval at her outfit. He carried a bag with him, and she wondered what manner of delights was inside. First, he pulled out a simple pen and pencil and described to her the importance of contracts and what they involved. He also went over some of the basic things he expected from any submissive. Aimee listened intently, her desire throbbing and growing the more she heard. In her own home, she found it much easier to surrender the role of boss and take on a new identity, the identity of a subservient slut.

Jack stood up, and with a snap of his fingers, he ordered Aimee to her knees. A deep instinctive part of her knew what he wanted even though he didn't say anything. It was as though she had a natural inclination to be submissive. Indulging it allowed her mind to flood with sensations. She sank to the floor, on her knees.

"Put your hands in your lap and open your mouth," he said. She did as ordered and looked up at him, feeling the saliva pool near her lips. He walked around her, describing how she was going to obey him and how he was going to take care of her, how he was going to push her limits and help her grow into her submission while she satisfied his sexual needs. Then, he stood in front of her. She watched as he unclasped his belt and pulled down his pants, revealing his manhood. He was in the prime of youth and his vigor rivaled that of a Greek god. If her mouth hadn't already been hanging open, it would have dropped of its own accord at the sight of the sweet thickness. He grabbed the back of her head in one of his huge hands and suddenly she felt very small. He pulled her head back and pain blurred with pleasure. Then she tasted him, his fervent tip resting against her tongue, his taut flesh sliding between her wet lips, the rush of tension through his body as he began to claim her. She closed her eyes, as she took him deeply into her throat, and felt the exhilaration of submission.

Jack had her head in his hand and he was controlling her movements. It was pure blissful joy to feel the movements of her body being controlled by someone else. She didn't need to think about anything, didn't need to do anything, she could just let him do what he needed to do. He thrust away, pounding her mouth, tearing away all inhibitions for she had never been used like this before.

A warm haze rose within her mind and fire crackled inside her. The sham of a life she had lived before was now being eroded away. Aimee instinctively reached up to touch his thigh and curl a hand around his manhood, but he slapped it away hard.

"I never told you to do that," he growled, pulling her away by the scruff of her neck. He threw her down. "Get on all fours," he said. She did as he asked and twisted her head back as he went to his bag and pulled out a leather flogger. He walked back to her to drag the flogger over her back. The leather caressed her skin, and then as he reached her rear, he brought his hand up and whipped the flogger down. She felt the rush of air before the impact, and her mouth hung open as she gasped from pain. It reverberated through her body, and an erotic song began to thrum over her flesh. Jack brought the flogger down again and again, and she could feel the deep red marks being etched into her skin from the bites of the leather.

Her head hung. The sensations were so intense that she was unable to form any coherent words. She looked back at Jack and saw his face twisted in pure delight. Something new had come over him, some primal, dominant energy, something that had been hiding within him all this time. It had only taken the small act of getting on her knees for her to see it. Now, he wasn't just a writer at her magazine. He was her Dominant, and whatever doubt she had was ripped away with every beat of the flogger.

Soon enough his hands were upon her again. He spanked her raw ass and then dragged his fingers down her inner thigh, which was slick and burning. She whimpered as he touched her without mercy, taking control of her body without any hesitation. She moaned and smiled and enjoyed the euphoric bliss that danced inside. He teased her, bringing the tips of his fingers so close, hovering over her clit, before he moved them across her legs and her stomach. Her body shuddered, and she begged him.

"You know how to be a good slut. You were born to be this way," he said in a low, commanding voice. Then all of a sudden his fingers were inside her, curling back and forth, getting deeper and deeper with every passing moment. He increased the tempo, drilling his fingers inside her, making erratic and wild bursts of pleasure rush through her mind. She felt the erotic bliss blooming and swelling. She closed her eyes as sweetness beckoned, only for Jack to tease her as he withdrew his fingers. They were soaked. She was certain she'd never been this wet before. He leaned forward and brought them to her mouth. She sucked them and tasted her own sex, her tongue sliding all over his fingers, before he brought them away and then replaced his fingers with his flogger. She clamped her lips around it.

"Don't drop it," he ordered, and she was determined to obey him. She gagged and it almost fell out straight away. He grabbed hold of her ass and squeezed firmly, before moving up to her. His manhood pressed against her, and then his thick erection was splitting her apart, plunging deep inside her. It took everything she had to hold the flogger in her mouth. She groaned and whimpered and then her body arched as Jack started to pound her. He went slowly, rhythmically at first, totally in control. She had no idea when he had gotten it, but then she felt her hands being tied together with rope behind her back. With nothing to support her, her head fell and the flogger stretched her cheeks, but still she clung on. She was nothing but a limp little toy, and she loved every single minute of it. This is what had been missing from her life. Her eyes rolled into the back of her head with exquisite happiness, as Jack fucked her from behind, taking control of her body and her mind; of everything she had.

It was an intense fuck. She had been brought so close to orgasm by his fingers that it didn't take much for everything to gush out of her in an intense burst, making her entire body quiver. Jack didn't seem to care and went at her with his face twisting in fury, keeping his hands clamped on her body until she felt his tension being released in one hot flow, mixing with her own mess. She felt delirious because she had somehow managed to keep hold of the flogger.

"You've done well. I think you have a lot of potential," Jack said after he'd finished panting and had wiped the sweat from his brow. He took the flogger from her, and she gasped for breath, her entire body still bubbling and

blazing. She begged to be able to play again and put on a
show for him, which he allowed.

***

After the heat had subsided and Aimee had cleaned herself
up, she came back to see Jack getting dressed again. The
contract was waiting for her to sign. Jack's name was
already on the paper.

"I added a condition as well, with your approval. I thought
it might be fun to write anonymously about our experiences
together. Everyone reading will get to know about how I'm
training you to be a naughty girl, and we'll be hiding in
plain sight," he said. Aimee's eyes widened at this
delicious thought. She eagerly took the pen and signed her
name.

"Well, that was just all kinds of wonderful," Aimee murmured, as she sighed heavily. All the tension in her body unspooled in that one breath, as she relaxed next to the younger, powerful man. Her arms were draped across his broad chest, her fingers sliding over the slick sweat that beaded on his taut skin. Her supple flesh was flushed with the lingering fire of arousal. Her soul had been opened and a radiant light poured out. For the first time in her life, she felt wholly satisfied. She was so small compared to him, fitting against him perfectly. His long arm reached around her and stroked her waist, holding her tightly, as though he owned her.

He did own her.

The wild passion she had experienced ran rampant through her mind and threatened to turn her on again. She'd always thought that only young women could be sluts, and that it was a derogatory term. But as Jack had been pounding away at her tight, wet pussy while whispering in her ear that she was *his* slut, the word had taken on a whole new meaning. Being on her knees for him—serving him, being used by him, agreeing to give herself to him completely— made her feel whole in a way that she never had before. Now, she knew why her marriage had failed. Now, she knew why she had never been satisfied in any relationship prior to this. It had been missing one vital component; BDSM.

She felt as though she was going to melt into a puddle of warm liquid next to him. She pressed her lips against his body and tasted his salty sweat.

"It was, indeed. You did well. I think you're a natural at pleasing your master," he said, leaning his head down and kissing her on the forehead, wiping away a few errant strands of matted hair. A smile played on Aimee's lips. *Her* master. The fact that someone wanted to own her, wanted to use her and train her and teach her how to be the perfect fuck-toy was just overwhelmingly beautiful. A sense of bliss rippled through her body. A haze filled her mind and she wanted the feeling to last forever.

"You were rougher than I expected. Like an animal," she said. Her body still throbbed with pain. She looked down at her flesh and saw the red marks he'd left. Like an apex predator, he had marked his territory and claimed her as his own. He had hunted her, clawed and bit and, at certain points, she had been afraid he would tear her apart completely, but that had only added to the excitement.

"Yeah, sorry about that. I tend to get carried away. It's just like a beast comes over me, and I can't stop myself," he ran a hand through his thick, tousled hair.

"You don't have to apologize. I like it. I just wish it didn't sting so much," she said. The marks on the back of her thighs and ass where he had flogged her stung as well. She had been used like a toy and now the pleasure had been burned away, she was left with the raw, throbbing pain.

"Do you have any lotion?" he asked. Aimee nodded and directed him to the bedroom, where she had a tube of lavender scented soothing lotion. He returned and squeezed a dollop onto his hands, rubbed it into his palms, and then applied it to her body. The cool sensation brought instant relief as his fingers roamed over her skin, rubbing it across the red marks.

"You look happy with yourself," she murmured, gasping as her eyes closed naturally.

"I just like admiring my handiwork." He turned her around when he was finished with her front so that he could do the same to her back.

"I never thought you'd have this gentle side to you."

"That's exactly why I wanted to write the column in the first place, because there are a lot of misconceptions about the world that I think should be brought up. You know, a lot of people think it's a scene for deviants and only psychos indulge in it, but it's just a healthy way to increase pleasure and share a strong bond with another person. And aftercare is one of the most important things. It's part of a Dom's duty to make sure his sub is looked after."

"Tell me more," she whispered as he massaged her lower back and thighs.

"Well, to be honest, when I was getting into the scene, I was smart enough to look at all the resources available, and I looked at the psychology of it first before I ever tried anything. I also spoke to a lot of experienced people, and they gave me a lot of help, but not everyone is that resourceful. Some people just fall into it, and it gives rise to their darker impulses without the structure of rules and limits. There was a point where I took it upon myself to mentor newcomers to the lifestyle because I was getting disappointed hearing about girls who thought being a submissive meant doing whatever the Dom wanted to do. There were so many people out there taking advantage of naïve women. It really annoyed me because it tarnishes what I think is a wonderful lifestyle, but I realized that I could only do so much. That's why I want to write this column."

"I think it's going to be a big hit. I wonder how many there are like me, who have these desires but don't even know it."

"Probably more than you think. I mean, think about how many divorces there are because people are dissatisfied with their relationship. Sometimes, you don't know what you're missing."

"I know now, and I have a lot of pleasure to catch up on," she said, twisting her body around when Jack was done to throw her arms around his neck and kiss him deeply. His arms slid down around her back, his strong arms not wavering in the slightest as he held her. Being so close to his naked body brought back the intense memories of the writhing and the panting, of the pleasure, and how she had descended into an insane world of lust and beautiful depravity. She broke off the kiss, throwing her head back into a laugh. She exposed the hollow of her throat. Her blonde hair fell against her shoulders, and her pert breasts shook as she laughed.

"What's so funny?" he asked.

"I just can't believe this has happened to me. It's such a big transformation. I mean, I'm here, with a junior writer, a man far too young for me. It's all so taboo, and yet I don't feel wrong about it at all."

"That's because there is nothing wrong. The only reason you feel like this is because our society has this weird love-hate relationship with sex. I mean, think about it, it's everywhere. Everything is sexualized especially in advertisements, but it's all made with images and innuendo. When it comes to actually talking about it in a mature and respectful way we always fail. It's no wonder that so many people go into their adult lives so confused. We're bombarded with sexual imagery from a young age, but then we have to figure it out for ourselves because we're too embarrassed to talk about it."

Aimee stopped laughing when she realized how serious he was taking his. She rested her head on the pillow and pulled him down to lay beside her again.

"I've never heard you sound so passionate about anything."

"It's important to me. I think it should be more important to everyone. Sex is such an important part of our lives and so many people don't reach their potential, or they practice things and end up getting hurt because they're not being responsible. All I want is for people to be safe and happy and for them to push their limits with someone they trust, not to be used by someone who isn't going to care about them at all."

Aimee caressed his cheek and kissed his chest affectionately.

"I'm so happy I have you as my Dom. I know I wouldn't want anyone else."

Jack closed his eyes and smiled, taking in a deep breath to try and calm down.

"It means a lot to me," he said. "Earning the trust and submission of a woman always gives me a surge of strength. I thrive on the power," he said. Hearing him talk like this made Aimee tingle.

"Is there anything else I can do for you Sir?" she asked, dipping her head in a submissive manner. She felt this need to obey ripple over her like a cloak and it pulled her down to where she was below him. She looked up, knowing that despite being his boss, he was now the superior and he controlled her body. If he asked her to do anything she would obey without hesitation, and she trusted that he would not ask anything of her that was too much for her to handle.

Jack shifted his body so that he was laying parallel to her. He placed his hand on her waist and moved so that he was within inches of her. She felt his warm breaths against her lips and found his musky, masculine scent to be intoxicating.

"I love that you're so willing to please me, but right now we need to talk about a few things. Now, do you want this to be a bedroom only thing or would you like it to seep out into the real world as well?"

"What do you mean? Like, me giving you blow jobs in my office?" Aimee asked. Jack chuckled, amused at her naivety.

"This lifestyle is not always about sex, at least, I don't prefer it to be that way. I like knowing that I have control in more ways than that, in more subtle ways. I want it to extend to regular life. I like the idea of hiding in plain sight, of displaying you as my submissive without anyone knowing."

"And how would you go about that?" Aimee asked.

Jack brought his hand up and dragged a single finger down the curves of her neck and side, leaving a trail of fire behind him, eventually resting on her wrist.

"There are ways. For example, I might tell you what to wear, or get you to wear a choker. I also like you marking your wrist with SLS. It stands for Sir's Little Slut, and it's an easy way for you to display that you're owned without having to actually tell anyone."

Aimee found the idea thrilling. "And what if anyone asks me what it stands for?"

"All you have to say is that it's there to remind you of something."

Aimee smiled wickedly. "I love that idea. Especially at work."

"Yes…work. I know that it might get a little complicated seeing as you're my boss. I will still do everything you ask, but as my submissive everything else is under my control. I want you to ask me for permission whenever you want to play with yourself. I want you to always be respectful and polite with me. Your body is mine and I want you to send me surprise pictures and videos so that I can create a gallery for my own enjoyment." He leaned in and lowered his voice. "I want to make you my personal porn star."

Heat twitched between Aimee's thighs and her mouth opened. A silent gasp burst out. She swallowed a lump in her throat. "I think I can do that," she whispered. Jack smiled and brushed his lips against hers.

"I want you to write about me," she said. It was a topic they had bandied about before they'd had sex as part of their flirting with each other, but now she was certain that she wanted it to happen. The thought of it turned her on and a vibrant haze rose within her mind, tingling and sparkling with a shimmering brilliance.

"Are you sure you don't want to keep what happens personal?"

"I love the idea of hiding in plain sight. It's going to be anonymous anyway, and the thought that millions of people are going to read about how you're training me to be your slut is just…oh it makes me tremble," she said, visibly shaking. "I want to look at that magazine and the articles online and feel proud that you've written about me."

"Then that is exactly what I'll do," Jack said, kissing her deeply this time, so deeply that she melted into him.

***

When the morning arrived, Aimee's body had recovered from the night of passion. The red marks had faded to crimson shadows. Jack awoke in response to her kisses and he smiled. She slid her fingers in between his and pressed her body close so there was nothing but heat between them. He was so young, so powerful she almost felt as though she didn't deserve to be with him, but he had chosen her and claimed her and he wouldn't like it if she had these thoughts. He wouldn't have taken her if he didn't think she was worth it.

"Let's go and clean up together," she whispered. Jack nodded and the two of them left the warmth of the bed. They were still naked, and she took great joy at looking at his body, which was like a work of art. Every inch of him was just perfect. It was as though he had been ripped from one of her fantasies and made real. In fact, she was afraid that she was still dreaming, and she would soon wake up to a life devoid of this passion.

She walked into the cubicle and turned on the faucet. Within a few moments, warm water poured out and, cascading in strong lines, hitting her skin. Steam rose and the cubicle door clicked shut behind her. She smiled as two strong arms came around her waist and roamed around her body. One went down to her thigh, the other groped her breasts, sliding around her slick, hard nipples. Water trickled down her body and fell down her face. Her hair thickened and grew heavy as it captured the water. Jack's hand curled around her throat and squeezed, the pressure was exquisite and her hands went limp. He tweaked and pinched her nipples, causing a rush of pleasure to burst through her body, before his hand ran up her inner thigh and touched the ache.

Her hands slammed against the cold tiles to steady herself. She panted loudly, her mouth hung open and warm water poured in. Jack's hands played with her, teasing her, finally entering her and curling back and forth. She surrendered to him. Pleasure swam through her blood. It flowed as easily as the water from the shower, as though all he had to do was turn on a faucet and she was instantly aroused. The biting water added to the sensations and it seemed to work in harmony with his hands and lips and teeth. She felt his heavy, hard body behind her, pressing into her, threatening her with all its ardent promise. She reached behind to try and grab him, but he batted her hand away.

"Not yet," he growled.

Then he took his hand away and she whimpered in frustration for she had been so close to bliss.

He took hold of her and turned her around, slammed her against the tiled wall. The shock of the cold blue tiles made her gasp, as did the impact. She had no time to process it, though, as he kissed her deeply and firmly, threatening to bruise her lips. His tongue was in her mouth and all she felt were his lips and the warm water. He reached down with his hand and lifted up her leg, grabbing it hard with one hand. Then, he set her down again and placed his hand around her neck. He snarled, possessed by the beast inside him. His eyes shone with desire and lust, a need for her, and she was all too happy to be the object of his desire and to give him what he needed.

He placed pressure on her neck and then he reached up and took hold of the shower head. He pushed it close to her and she felt the pulsing water travel all down her body, until it was focused between her thighs. Her head arched back as the sensations were focused on the most intimate part of her body. Her entire body shuddered and trembled as it felt like a thousand whips were dancing around her. Her knees buckled and Jack could sense this.

"Get on your knees," he ordered, and she obeyed without hesitation. The cascading water hit her breasts and then she gasped as the temperature changed to a shocking cold. Her arms wrapped around her defensively and she screamed. The warmth returned. She looked up at Jack, who pursed his lips.

"Open your mouth." She did as she was told and took his rampant thick Dom cock. She sucked hard as he held the shower head to her face, the biting water snapping at her like piranhas. Her lips wrapped around his wet erection as his free hand took hold of her matted hair, taking control of her head, fucking her face. Her saliva mixed with the water as he thrust himself deep inside her, wrecking her lips and making a slut of her. Her eyes rolled into the back of her head. The shower was a place to get clean, but she was just getting dirtier with every passing moment. Her sense of self was driven away from her. In this moment she was nothing but his slut, his submissive, his toy, and she loved it.

He took his erection and smeared it across her face, wiping away the wetness of the water with it. Jack shoved the showerhead against her mouth and she gagged on the water. It poured back out of her in spurts and spits before she was filled with his erection again. She looked up through bleary eyes and saw his powerful body towering over her, so tall and strong. He was superior to her, and she was beneath him, where she knew she belonged.

Jack reached behind her and twisted the faucet. In one easy moment, the shower was silenced and the only sounds were his grunts, her muffled moans, and the sound of his erection slapping her lips.

He pulled himself away and kept hold of her head, dragging her out of the cubicle. He threw her out of the door, tossing her to the ground. She landed on the plush carpet, dripping wet, her body making a dark outline on the floor. He took a towel and wrapped it tightly around her face, masking her. He pulled the ends and held them in one hand, making her neck strain back as though she was a horse and he was holding her reins. It was overwhelming and blitzing. For a moment, she wasn't sure she could take it, but then he was inside her and everything was complete. Her body was bending to his will.

He thrust powerfully, releasing everything inside her. All his passion and dark lust fueled his movements. His body slammed against hers, pumping her hard. She bit down on the towel, eyes closed as she felt him getting deeper and deeper inside her, reaching the most elusive part of her and everything blazed within. A warm glow gorged itself on their passion, and it grew into a great flame, burning as brightly as a super nova.

Jack was rampant.

The loving man who had tended to the care of her body had once again unleashed the beast upon her. He didn't stop until his body rocked and convulsed, and she descended into the yawning abyss. A long, guttural grunt shot through his body, and then he released her. The towel dropped from her mouth and she heaved in air. Collapsing to the floor, her arms splayed out. She looked up at Jack. His muscles glistened and his chest moved fiercely, as the beast slipped away from him and he returned to his normal, calm state.

"I just couldn't resist you," he said. Aimee lay her head back on the floor and laughed, surrendering to the intoxicating elation of it all.

***

After they'd dried and dressed, they went downstairs and prepared for the day. They'd already agreed to go to work separately to not arouse any suspicion. The last thing Aimee wanted was to lose her job. As much as she was willing to give herself to Jack, she wasn't prepared to give up everything she had worked hard for, nor would he expect her to. They both valued their careers, so it was important for them to not get carried away and to keep things under control.

"I'll draw up a contract for you to sign to make this official, so that we know what our limits are and how we're going to move forward. Before I leave, there's something I need to do." He reached over to grab a pen, and then took her wrist. He pushed up the sleeve of her blazer and wrote SLS on her wrist in deep black ink, marking her. Seeing him write this made her go weak at the knees. She looked at it, feeling honored.

"I love it. It looks perfect," she said. He pulled her close and kissed her tenderly.

"It's not only there to remind you that your owned, it's also a symbol of strength. If you ever feel like you're doubting yourself or you're worried, you can look down at your mark and remind yourself that you are owned. That you have been chosen, and you should derive strength from this. I'll see you at work, and I'll get working on the column.

Aimee was left reeling. Everything had been transformed. She now saw the world in a different way. Her eyes had been opened, and it was as though she had been baptized. Now that she was aware of all these things she wondered how many other people in her life had been interested in the same things. She wondered if her past relationships would have gone differently had she expressed an interest in these taboo desires. When she left, she looked at strangers and wondered about the dark desires in their minds. The whole word was a breeding ground for taboo kinks and she had now shorn away the trappings of society. She was free of the shackles and she absolutely loved it.

***

Before she went into work, Aimee spent a few moments composing herself. She couldn't allow anyone to guess that anything untoward had happened between her and Jack. She also couldn't let her submissive nature creep into her job. She was the editor, she called the shots, she was in charge. This indulgence of her submissive tendencies threatened to have a disruptive effect on her career. She had just spent the night and the morning serving Jack and she had to willfully snap out of that mood and return to the responsibilities she held dear. There would be a phone call with Greg for sure, and other decisions had to be made. She couldn't afford to doubt herself or hesitate.

But when she entered work, it was as though her personality was tied to the place. As soon as she stepped into the office, she shed the need to be submissive for her editorial personality and commanded the authority of the room. It helped that nobody apart from Jack knew of her secret desire, and he hadn't arrived yet. She told herself that things would be just fine.

She made her way to her office and set down her bag. She sat down her jacket, rose and caught a glimpse of her mark, and then smiled.

First, she checked her emails. There was an impatient one from Greg. She had already promised him that a captivating article would be appearing on the website, and it would change the fortunes of the magazine. She hoped she hadn't overstated people's desire to learn about BDSM. It had changed her life in such a short space of time, and she hoped she wasn't just projecting.

She glanced at the phone and knew she couldn't put it off for too much longer. Greg was going to be angry, but she had handled him when he had been angry before. It was better to get this over with, otherwise it would cast a pall over the day.

She picked up the phone and dialed his number. He answered almost instantly.

"Ah Aimee, I've been waiting for some news. Where is this article you promised me?"

"It's going to be coming later today, and it's going to be worth the wait."

"It better be," he snarled, "because, if it's not, I'm holding you responsible. Your job is to make this magazine worth my time and money. If you can't, then I'm going to pull the plug. You'd better hope this anonymous gambit of yours works. Are you sure this writer can be trusted?"

"Yes, it's just that it's a delicate subject matter, and he doesn't want anyone to know his identity because there are still some ignorant opinions about the things he's writing about."

"Yes, well, I think that's a guarantee when you're talking about whips and chains and all that kind of thing. This better be tasteful, Aimee. I'm not going to peddle smut."

"You have my word Greg. You won't regret it," she looked down at her mark to gain the patience to speak with him.

"I want a proof of it as soon as you get it, and get it up on that website as soon as possible. I've been getting an earful from the marketing manager about how we're not getting enough traffic. We need to get more eyeballs on our site."

"I promise you'll have it, Greg. How long have I done this job? I've never let you down before," she said sharply. Greg sighed.

"See to it you don't ever let me down," he said before ending the call. Aimee put the phone back down and rubbed her temples. It had been easy to lose herself in a world of submission and sex, and she thought it no wonder that she wanted to escape when she had so much stress in her life. All she wanted was to switch off and lose herself, but in this office it was impossible. She looked out at the writers and the administrators. It was only a small office, but each of them worked hard. It was such a competitive industry that jobs were like gold dust. If the magazine failed, it was unlikely that they would get jobs in the industry again. Because of her experience, Aimee might be able to survive, but she didn't want to risk it. Everything was riding on this article, on Jack's idea, and she hoped that she hadn't misplaced her faith in him.

How could she, though, when he was her dominant? It shamed her that she would even doubt him for one moment.

She read through a few more articles that other people had written and made a few changes to make them the best that they could be. It was difficult to concentrate, though, for her mind was on her journey into submission. All she wanted was to leave this life behind and throw herself into the world that Jack inhabited.

He came in about half an hour after she arrived. She looked up and smiled. A tingle twitched inside her, but she quelled the instinct because she had to remain professional. She couldn't allow her personal relationship to bleed into the professional realm. Jack caught her eyes, and there was a flash of a smile. It was enough to give her strength to carry on.

She saw him typing frantically, away from the others so that nobody could see what was on his screen. It filled her with excitement to know that he was writing about her and their experiences together. It was so dangerous as well. If anyone should suspect anything…her gaze darted around the office to check that nobody was curious. They were all too focused on their own jobs and their own lives. They wouldn't even conceive that something like this could happen.

Because she needed to keep Jack's identity a secret, he was going to email the article to her from a secondary account, and he was also going to work on another article so people didn't suspect that he was the anonymous source. It meant that he had to double his workload, but he was happy to do it because it meant so much to him. He was truly a caring man and, although he had a primal, savage side, it was clear that he was thoughtful and wanted to take care of her. She felt safe with him and pitied the women who weren't so lucky to find such a mentor. How many vulnerable young women were out there, eager to experience this lifestyle, but lacking the teacher? And how many men were waiting to prey on them, calling themselves Doms, but only concerned with their own pleasure. It would have been easy for other people to fall through the cracks and become scarred by their experiences, linking them to BDSM when in fact it was because they had been taught improperly.

She could only imagine what it might have been like for her, eager to learn, willing to give herself at the first time of asking to someone who seemed like he knew what they were talking about when, in reality, they were just a fraud and only wanted her for the thrill of sexual pleasure. She had been fortunate that Jack had found her and was willing to guide her. Not everyone would be the same, but at least with this article it might help raise awareness and people might be a little more discerning when it came to indulging their forbidden desires with sexual partners. It wasn't just a way to save the magazine; she hoped it would save a few people as well.

Jack was right when he said that there the lack of knowledge endangered people. It wasn't as though anyone could lead a class on this thing as well, so she hoped that the right people read this article and it would spread some good as well as bring revenue in.

***

At one point in the afternoon, Jack rose from his desk and knocked on her office. She called him in, and he shut the door behind him. Tension filled the air and she felt the urge to throw herself at him, an urge she resisted with everything she had for she did not want to fall into a trap where she was weak around him all the time.

"I have the article for you. It might be a little rough because it all came out in one stream of consciousness, so you might have to tidy it up. I tried to change my style a little as well so that people can't identify me, although I doubt it will matter to too many people to try. I have something for you to sign as well."

He slid over a few sheets of paper. Aimee checked her email and saw that the article had popped up. She opened the paper and saw that it was a contract he had prepared.

"We can go over specific limits later, but for now that should cover anything. It's a standard contract. I've already signed it. I'll leave it with you to read and you can get it back to me later. It's a matter of safety, you know? Everything is laid out there so there's not going to be any miscommunication and nobody is going to get hurt or do anything the other person is uncomfortable with."

The contract made everything so real. Aimee nodded and thanked him. He rose, not wanting to linger in her office for too long for tongues to start wagging. Aimee loved spending time with him, loved the thought of being his submissive, but a contract seemed so official. It wasn't legal, obviously, it was something more personal and it was good that things could be laid out in such a way to keep things safe and consensual. Her heart beat firmly in her chest as she read it, knowing that, if she signed it, she was committing herself to this lifestyle and all that it entailed for the foreseeable future.

She set it aside for the moment, unsure if she was ready to put pen to paper. She was more eager to look at the article. She wasn't entire sure what to expect from Jack's writing, but it turned out to be something heartwarming and honest. He wrote about his struggles to fit in, the way he had always been confused when he wasn't as satisfied in relationships as he should have been, or the way he had these dark impulses that seemed wrong. He spoke about how he learned more, and how he made mistakes, and how he wanted to write this article to prevent others from making the same mistakes. Then, he started talking about Aimee and everything they had done together. Reading it in black and white and hearing how it had felt for him brought her closer, made everything more intimate. She knew how powerful the sensations were for herself, but she hadn't even begun to think that he felt the same transcendent things.

All this time, she had been focused on what this dynamic meant for her, and she realized that she had been thinking about Jack as a tool. But in this article, she began to see how a Dom needed a submissive just as much as the submissive needed a Dom. It was symbiotic relationship. It had been selfish of her to only think of herself. To know that she meant so much with him filled her with more than lust, with more than sexual desire, and she quickly became aware that this agreement was more than just a way to indulge sexual kinks. It was a partnership, an agreement to share intimacy with each other and trust each other with everything they had.

The article did titillate her, for it was thrilling. Her exploits would be there for everyone to read without anyone knowing it was really her, but it had a deeper meaning as well. She wanted to take care of Jack just as much as he wanted to teach her. It was his job to please her and guide her through submission, but it was her duty to support him and make sure that he never felt anything less than loved and worshipped.

As soon as she finished reading the article, she pulled out the contract and put pen to paper, signing her name wherever it needed signing. She was ready and willing to give herself to Jack in every possible way. To make the contract more personal, she brought it to her lips, puckered her mouth, and left an echo of lipstick on the paper. This contract meant the world to her, and she would do everything she could to fulfill her role as a submissive.

She turned back to the computer and, with a smile on her face, began to edit the article to make it ready for publication. And then, it would be time to give Jack material to write the next one. The thought made her eyes gleam with wicked, mischievous delight.

Anne Lawther, a lady in her mid-twenties with fair hair and pale skin, had always had a timid disposition. But her eyes sparkled brightly, and her mind was inquisitive. She wore a white frock that spoke to her innocence and the only piece of jewelry she owned; a locket that her dearly departed mother had given her. It rested against her chest and rose with every breath. She sat on deck as she ventured towards lands unknown. When she had decided to leave the comforting home of England, she hadn't properly prepared herself for such a long journey.

She had received an invitation from one of her cousins to visit his home in a paradise on a faraway island. The thought, at first, had struck her as too dangerous and wild, yet something in her heart had called to her. Life in England was not turning out as she had expected. While she had many suitors, none of them seemed appropriate. A lot of pressure was placed upon her to live life in a manner that was expected rather than in a way that she wanted.

These radical ideas and philosophies she kept to herself. So far, she had been able to avoid marriage even though it should have happened many years ago. Now, horrible rumors were being spread by the men she had spurned, rumors that had made her flee. Just thinking of them made tears sting her eyes. Oh, how cruel men could be! She saw the way they looked at her. Often, she feared that their lust and hunger would get the better of them. She had learned that men had animalistic urges, and they had to release them at some point. It was a credit to their discipline that they had managed to control themselves.

However, even though she was ashamed to admit it to herself, a deep part of her wanted them to lose control and ravish her. Although Anne was timid by nature, she had often wondered what it would be like to lose herself in the arms of a strong man. Every time these thoughts thundered through her mind, she trembled and flushed with embarrassment, ever afraid that somebody would find out the truth.

She knew it was sinful, yet her need brought such powerful desire and temptation; it would be impossible to resist. Anne wondered if she was an evil person, if her soul had been tainted by the devil himself. She prayed nightly for the Lord to rid her of these temptations, but He never did.

The ship, called *Freedom*, sloshed through the waves of the open sea. For most of their journey, the skies had been blue and cloudless, and the sea had shimmered under the golden sun like a glass blanket. Occasionally, they had also seen wondrous creatures leaping from the sea. Anne's mouth had dropped with astonishment each time.

Her life had been somewhat sheltered in England. Now, she was beginning to realize that the world was a much larger place than she had ever imagined. Her excitement now outweighed her fear. She was looking forward to seeing the life her cousin lived. From the letters she received, he seemed to live a life he wanted. He traded in rum and spices and had paid for her fare from England, seemingly having endless amounts of money. She owed him much and looked forward to repaying the debt.

When she had boarded the ship, she had always assumed she would return to England after some time. Now that she had been at sea for a while, she wondered if she would ever return. There was little waiting for her in that dreary country. Her cousin had shown her that it was possible to forge a life, a good life, away from all she had known.

Archie had been a rascal in his youth. Everyone bemoaned the way he lived his life as they were sure he would fall in with a disreputable crowd. However, he had seized an opportunity to leave, one obviously beneficial for him. Anne hoped that she would also find the same kind of opportunity.

The days passed. She read books and spent time looking out towards the sea. She had made some friends on the crew who had taught her games of chance and a few bawdy songs. Over the course of the journey, she had become a lot more relaxed around them and found them to be good company, if not a little rough around the edges.

But the voyage was not destined to be a peaceful one. Dark, roiling clouds drifted across the sky, creating a murky vista where, once before, there had been nothing but a clear blue horizon. Shadows fell upon them, and the sky boomed with rumbles of thunder. Lightning, alive and furious, cracked like a whip and flashed among the clouds. Rain came down in heavy drops, smashing and splattering against the deck which made the surface slippery.

The sea churned as powerful winds came rushing through and knocked more than one sailor off their feet, sadly knocking some overboard. Anne, struggling to maintain her balance, heard their flailing screams but was unable to do anything to help them. Her hands reached for purchase, but they slipped away from the boat. Every inch of her soon became wet; her frock clung to her skin, and her hair matted to her face.

When she looked up at the storm, she was filled with awe and fear. It seemed inexorable and filled her vision. There was no escape.

The sea was foamy and churned, violently rocking the boat. The sailors scrambled for safety, and she could hear yells as they tried to stabilize the boat. The world was a blur. Someone called out to her to get to safety. A rough pair of hands grabbed her, and she squealed. They carried her a few feet, but part of the sail swung around, and she head a crack. The man beside her fell.

She screamed as the boat turned to the side. Losing her footing, she crawled to the side of the boat and, gripping the wooden beams tightly, hung on for dear life. Rain slashed down and, as the lightning flashed, it illuminated the boat. She saw what carnage the storm had wrought; men lay dying, and the boat was cracked and splintered. The sail was tattered and torn.

Freedom groaned under its own weight. Anne could feel the world moving underneath her. Her tears mixed in with the rain streaming down her cheeks, and her fervent fearful screams were lost amid the wild sounds of the storm.

The destructive storm seemed to have come from nowhere and was paying no heed to all her hopes and dreams. Her journey had only just begun, but now it was coming to an end. She prayed for forgiveness as the lightning struck the boat again. Flames rose, licking the wet wood, but soon turned to smoke again.

The sailors' yells turned more desperate. Did they feel as helpless as she did against such a force of nature? The volume of their shouts had been diminished as well since there were fewer of them alive or on board. Anne twisted around and, in the darkness, she could see a few vague shapes bobbing about. She gulped, for she knew that the same fate awaited her.

As a single bolt of lightning illuminated the boat once again, she caught the gaze of another sailor. The same fear was reflected on his face as she felt in her own heart. Time seemed to stand still for that moment as she realized that he was probably going to be the last man she ever saw alive.

Suddenly, she was fraught with anxiety, and her soul was filled with regret for the life she had not lived. The sailor opened his mouth as if to say something, but the light faded as another boom of thunder crashed around them. She searched the darkness for him, but he was gone.

Another mighty crack sounded around her and made a huge rent in the boat. It leered to the side. Anne managed to keep her grip even though the boat buckled underneath her. The sea tossed it about heartlessly, as though it were playing with a toy. The fear of death struck her. She was utterly helpless and bereft of hope.

Her only recourse was to have faith that the Lord, in all His wisdom, would show mercy on her soul.

Darkness was her world now. She groaned and spat out rainwater. Her body ached all over, and she didn't know for how much longer she could hold on. She couldn't hear anyone else and assumed that she was the last one left alive. The boat shuddered, and more lightning forked down. Turbulent waves shook the boat, forming cracks in the wood around her.

It was only a matter of time now. Her tears joined the rain. She closed her eyes, weeping fretfully, and held on with all her remaining strength. Soon enough, they were lost in the sea as the relentless storm ripped the boat apart.

Plunging into the cold, dark depths, her heart was seized with utter, incomprehensible fear. As the water rushed around her, she knew nothing but darkness.

***

Anne awoke with a huge, gasping breath followed by a violent cough. She looked around at the calm water and blinked, wondering if she really was alive. She took a few moments to check that she had all her faculties and that she was unharmed. She seemed intact, which was a miracle. But where was she?

The storm had disappeared and, once again, she was surrounding by a peaceful sky and a calm sea. She bobbed along, resting on a wide piece of wood that stayed afloat. A few bits of debris floated around her. She strained to see if there were any other survivors or if the ship itself had stayed intact, but there was nothing.

But then…

She squinted in the distance and paddled forward a little bit. Her vision was hazy and, just for a moment she thought she might be hallucinating, but then she saw it. Land!

Anne was weak, but she used what remained of her strength to paddle through the cold water toward land. Thankfully, the current aided her. She thanked the Lord for showing her mercy and for giving her salvation from the storm. She mourned the rest of the crew, for it didn't seem as though they had survived.

Her struggles weren't over yet; for she was stranded, alone in this strange world and there was no telling how she was going to survive. Her stomach groaned, and her throat ached. Her clothes were torn, exposing different parts of her body. She appeared to have been vomited up by the sea.

She had no idea where she was or if anyone else, other than the crew, was around her. How cruel that abundant water sloshed by her sides, yet she couldn't quench her thirst. She groaned and her arms trembled, as she pushed her makeshift raft onwards.

Water spilled onto the surface and the sun beat down, making her feel even more tired and limp. Eventually, she managed to reach land. She groped at the sandy shore to pull herself out of the sea. Greatly relieved to be on land again, she lay flat on her back with her limbs splayed out on all sides. Grains of sand fell through her fingers and she laughed, for it was the only response that seemed natural to everything she had endured.

After some time, Anne summoned what little strength she had left and pushed herself up. She looked up and down the beach. It was beautiful; the sand undisturbed and the water lapped against the shore. Before her stood lush trees with thick trunks and, from these, hung colorful fruits. Her mouth watered at the thought of eating something fresh and juicy again. She licked her cracked, dry lips and moved forward, reaching out towards the fruit. Then, she stopped in her tracks.

Fear struck her as people emerged from the forest. They were clad in simple cloth, covering only parts of their body. Their skin was as dark as the night, and they had white paste in patterns over their flesh. They were all muscular and holding spears while they pointed at her.

Maybe she had been too hasty in thanking the Lord for her deliverance. She glanced back at the shore and turned on her heels. Her first instinct was to run and flee from these barbarians, but the sand was thick and her legs were weak. As she turned, her feet heavy stumbled and she fell to her knees.

She looked up as shadows fell upon her and saw the cruel faces of these tribal men. They didn't use words, only sounds by clacking their teeth and lips together. She pleaded with them, but her words meant nothing. She fought and struggled to get away but, even if she had been at full strength, she wouldn't have been able to resist. Anne was held aloft and dragged away, taken into the depths of the forest where these savage men lived.

Her feet bounced painfully along the dirty floor. The air was humid and sweat prickled against her skin. She twisted her head around, and her fervent gaze darted about. Trying to piece together the land she now inhabited, she hoped against hope to find some way to escape.

It certainly wasn't like the island that had been described to her by her cousin. This was one of those islands that she had read about; islands where the Lord's word hadn't reached, islands where primitive tribes did as they pleased and worshiped heathen gods. She knew she faced danger. She almost wished that the storm had taken and delivered her into the Lord's arms.

The sweetness of salvation turned bitter almost immediately.

The thick forest opened to a small settlement. A fire burned in the middle, and the air shimmered as flames licked the wood. Other members of their tribe looked at her with curiosity. Wearing the same scant strips of cloth, the women's breasts were exposed.

Shame and embarrassment for their immodesty filled Anne. None of them showed her any sign of kindness. Small huts surrounded the fire where meat was cooking, which stimulated her hunger. The heavy hands and tight grips of the tribesmen took her past the fire and into a hut at the rear of the camp. A curtain made of animal hide momentarily blanketed her face and body. Dragged inside, she was thrown to the ground.

Anne raised her head to view her surroundings. A man sat in an ornamental chair made of twisted bones and branches. He had a necklace made of animal teeth around his neck. She could only assume these were from wild beasts he had killed. From the number on show, he was clearly a formidable warrior.

From her vantage point, he towered above her. His body was taut and tight with muscle; every sinew on his arm was visible, and veins rippled along his supple, hairless obsidian skin. His lips were thick and smooth, his hands large, and his shoulders broad. Something about him seemed ageless as well, as though he had always lived and he always would. He rose from his bony throne, forcing her head to tilt back. He was as a giant compared to her.

He communicated with his men in deep clacks, the sounds as rumbling and powerful as the thunder of the storm. Although his presence made fear ripple through her body, something savage and primal spoke to the deepest part of her.

The air seemed to thrum with his masculine strength and vitality. Breath caught in her throat as he stood above her; a giant, a titan, a man who commanded respect and attention simply by acting as though it was his right. Awe gripped her as completely as the majestic aura of this king.

He cupped her chin in his hand and moved her head from left to right, and then ran his fingers through her hair. She gasped a little from his inspection. Was he checking to see if she was worthy of him?

She couldn't take her eyes off him, but they lowered as if beckoned by the object of his masculinity. A thin piece of cloth hung over his groin. Her eyes widened, her gaze hanging on that stunning part of him; for it was huge and barely hidden by the small cloth.

Her heart raced even faster, but she didn't know why. She told herself to stop, to push those sinful thoughts aside. Her skin betrayed her, prickling with tension. This must be an instinctive reaction on her part, something that couldn't be challenged. At least, that's how her mind reasoned.

Snapping his fingers, the King directed his men to leave. Anne stayed on the floor, a miserable wretch, wondering what punishment this tribal chief had in store for her. She imagined that he had never seen anything like her before. Would she be treated like a commodity? Like a strange beast to be hunted and conquered?

The king gazed at her, squeezing her chin and forcing her to look up at him. Her gaze threatened to waver under his countenance. When he let go, her head dropped. She was too weak and tired to hold it up. He turned his back to her and walked to the side of the room. When he returned, he handed her a large fruit with mottled and tough skin. Anne tried to pierce it with her thumb, but she lacked the strength necessary.

Taking it from her, the king broke it open with his bare hands. Juice glistened on his fingertips. He handed her one half of the fruit which was bright inside and smelled sweet. Although loathe to give him any sign that she was at ease with being held prisoner, she couldn't resist the hunger gnawing at her stomach. She took the fruit eagerly and buried her face in it. Juice streamed down her chin as she gorged on it. Then, discarding the rough outer skin, she grabbed the other half. When she had finished, she wiped her hands on her frock.

"Thank you," she gasped.

He tilted his head.

"You don't understand a word I'm saying, do you?" she asked.

The king clacked something in reply, and her mood grew more somber. There would be no way of reasoning with him. She was completely at his mercy, although he had at least shown some tenderness by giving her the fruit. She felt better for having eaten. Her strength was now returning.

Yet she was still on her knees.

The king held out his hand. She had no choice but to take it. His skin was leathery and calloused, the sign of a man who had lived in the wild all his life. Her skin was delicate in comparison; her hand meek and small. Even while standing, he towered above her. Her head only reached his stomach. Temptation flared in her mind again, that rush of excitement which she tried so hard to will away.

She was a lady, meant to marry a gentleman, not to feel these sorts of things for a primitive tribal chief. But his muscles and his aura made focusing difficult. She was in thrall to him.

His hands were suddenly upon her, tearing away her tattered clothes which barely clung to her body. He ripped them apart and discarded them as if they offended him. It all happened so quickly that she barely had time to react. When she looked down at her nakedness, embarrassment heated her skin more strongly than the tropical air.

Her hand flung out, but her slap barely registered. He snarled but didn't even flinch at the impact. She tried slapping him again, but he caught her slender wrist and held her back. Fear tinged with excitement exploded from her stomach and made her gasp.

What was happening to her? Sure he was strong and mighty, but…

She was tired of thinking, tired of worrying about the woman she should be. All her life, she had tried to fight against the urges that flashed through her mind and tormented her body. Such sinful temptations! Where had resisting them gotten her?

Lost in a storm and shipwrecked on an island, that's where.

All because she'd been forced to flee cruel men who had spread vicious rumors about her maidenhood. They had proven themselves completely unworthy of her hand or her love. Now she stood before this king; an utterly dominating presence who sparked a deep lusty fire inside her.

She had skated so close to death that, during her fight to live, all she found in her life had been regret. She must live life, lest it disappear as fast as the ship had disintegrated when facing the storm. She silently vowed to follow her desires. She was tired of her self-constraint which had reduced her to living a lie. Even if the Lord had eyes on the world, He may not be watching this island.

Fear of death had freed her from ideas on the way she was supposed to live. Standing before this great, hulking man, her blood simmered with passion. She looked at her pale white arm held by his hard black fingers, and arousal gripped her even stronger than his hand clamped around her wrist.

When she met his gaze, understanding passed between them both. Who needed words when they had their bodies, their hearts, and their souls?

Anne ran her tongue over her lips and arched her neck back. The tribal king gazed at her naked body and smiled. A thrill passed through her. His smile said he deemed her worthy of him. He still held her arm with one hand, but the other traced a line downward from her cheek to her breast. He splayed his hand on her chest and seemed fascinated by their contrasting complexions. But then, so was she.

Thoughts of being taken by this dark-skinned savage king went against everything she had been taught as a well-behaved Christian girl from England. Temptation fired the deepest part of her; the part that ached for freedom.

His long, thick fingers ran down her body and cupped her breast. A small moan released from her as unfamiliar sensations darted here and there. He circled her nipple and squeezed, his hands so large and commanding. Her lungs dragged in air to full capacity. She felt so small, so vulnerable when held in his grip, but somehow she knew she would be safe with him.

He made nonsensical sounds as his eyes drank in her body while his hands went ever lower, resting against her chest and thigh. She quivered with anticipation, shifting her stance as wet heat prickled in the delta between her thighs. The king's hand drew back up her body, searing her skin with his effortless touch. He was already treating her body as if he owned her, and she wasn't going to do anything to disparage him of that notion.

His finger ran underneath the metal chain of her locket, tracing the thin band which usually rested against her neck. Suddenly, with one flick of his wrist, he tore it away. The locket bumped her skin like a parting kiss as he tossed the last link she had to her old life away.

She had never given a thought to how she would feel if the last vestige of civilized society that shackled her was ripped away. He had no regard for her place in society. Now, shorn of her reputation and her position as a lady, she cared nothing for it as well.

The king stepped back and pointed to the ground. Anne hesitated for a moment, but then sank to her knees and submitted to him. Although there was nothing she could do to resist, a swell of pleasure rose within her as she descended to the ground. The powerful gesture felt as though her soul was being released while vibrant energy slashed through her mind. Desire left her mind hazy and, even though it might seem wrong, she knew this was what she needed; this was where she belonged.

Steeping to his throne, the king then returned with what she thought was a whip. Her mind sizzled with anticipation, but he unfurled something completely different. It was a collar with a leash attached.

The thick twine scratched against her skin, as he placed it tightly around her neck. The act induced a sense of deliriousness. He held the leash in his hand, claiming her, which must have been some sort of rite for this tribe. Now, she belonged to the chief. Spat from the sea, she was now one with the island but claimed by this magnificent king.

She was flattered and awed, even after having everything stripped away from her. She would make him happy as his pure being of lust. In return, she knew he would take her to the edge of her limits. He pulled the course twine to the left, prickling a path across her neck and sending her senses in disarray. She'd had no clue of these realms of pleasure and delight, but she was sure that this king would take her places that no man in the world could match.

He tugged sharply at the leash and pleasure blazed through her once again. She looked up at him, submission heavy in her eyes, as every fiber of her being screamed a need to please him. Her fingers ached to worship his powerful body while her skin burned with want for him to teach her. So many naughty temptations throughout the years now flashed across her mind, sending fervent delight racing through her blood. She had to struggle not to squirm under her newfound acceptance of sin and depravity.

The king's hand moved around her scalp to hold her tightly, while his will upon her was irrevocable and resolute. She reached up and stroked his thigh, then reached for his swollen arousal. It was so large and threatened to tear through the cloth that provided the meekest of restraint. He peeled away that cloth and unleashed himself upon her.

So large and thick, Anne's eyes widened at the sight of him. He was impressive and every inch of him was in proportion with his titanic frame. The tip was smooth, the skintight and rippling with veins. A small bed of hair rested at the end of the shaft.

She had never been filled with such desire. Her past had been a pretense. Only now, she could embrace her true nature, her true destiny.

The king moved forward and held her head back. Anne's mouth dropped open, and she closed her eyes as he thrust his erection in between her wet, warm lips. She sucked on him, gorged on him as desperately as she had the fruit he had given her earlier. Her desire to serve him was as strong as her desire to survive. Muffled moans, obscured by the thick cock filling her mouth, escaped her lips. Her tongue swirled and tasted the musky sweetness of his sex. Soon enough, he was glistening with her saliva.

The fingers of both hands surrounded him. She slowly opened her eyes to see the corded muscles of his lower stomach. Tracking those muscles upward, her mouth didn't pause as her eyes roamed his massive frame. She loved how his body bristled with tension and his lips curled in a snarl. She pulsed between her legs as his tip repeatedly sank into her throat. Tightening her lips around him, she never wanted to let go.

As she pleasured him, she wondered if the desire he felt was as fierce as the one that swam through her blood. Moments later, she had her answer. His grip tightened on her scalp. So much so that she gasped in pain. He batted her hands away and held onto her head, and then slammed his erection into her mouth at a rhythm of his choosing.

Anne was taken aback, but her shock only lasted momentarily. She was driven by a deep need to serve. If this was what he needed to make him feel good, then it was what she was going to give him. Her cheeks flushed and her jaws ached as he roared a primal, animalistic sound. She continued to moan, growing louder every moment as her body responded to his; shaking and shuddering as her ache grew ever fiercer

She had heard tales and gossip; rumors and clandestine speak about what happened between a man and a woman. She had never experienced it for herself, thus she had no idea what to expect. She hoped she was doing well. By his reaction, she certainly seemed to be, but she was only doing what came naturally. It all felt so right. She instinctively knew just where and how to touch him. He smeared his erection over her face, across her tongue, and down her jawbone. Then, he held her body back and slapped his thick erection against her chest, cracking it as loud as a whip. Both admired their contrasting skin tones with every sharp, wet slap of his cock across her breast.

Then, he wrapped the leash around his fist and dragged her to the floor. She crawled on her hands and knees before he tugged with all his might and sent her sprawling down to where she was laying curled up, completely at his mercy. He kneeled, tugging the leash in one hand to obviously show her that he was in control. He dragged his other finger down the middle of her body and began to move it around her sweetest spot, the spot that she had always been so afraid to touch.

She gasped wildly as a sizzling heat robbed all thoughts from her mind. She writhed and clawed at the ground, breath rushing out of her in huge, heaving moans. Pleasure and pain passed through her as his expert fingers deftly moved around and inside her. He pulled at the leash, making her body arch uncomfortably, twisting this way and that while his other hand wicked maintained control of her. His long fingers slid and teased, seemed everywhere at once, before thrusting inside her so deeply that she was sure he reached her very soul.

Driven to delirium, with her legs parted wide and the collar bit at her neck, she looked down through blurred vision to see his fingers sliding in and out of her. So intimate. So connected. All her nerves had gone from pain to singing in pleasure as he rocked her from the intensity of his violent passion. The air sizzled with the king's dominating heat and she knew that she was his forever more. Although she had no experience previous to being with him, all that mattered was that she continued to be subjected to his whims and desires.

He growled and snarled like an animal, still rock hard, yet he seemed content to play with her. He leaned over and suckled on her breasts, biting and nibbling her nipples, then he moved up to the rest of her body. His hot breath washed over her, and his lips came down on hers. He pulled even more pleasure from her body. She cried out while trying to brace herself against the cacophony of delight that was raging through her body and mind, but he had control of her. Everything was so overwhelming and intoxicating. Her spirit felt as though it was rising from her body.

He swung his powerful frame atop her and moved her legs away. His hands clasped her body like a doll. With animalistic intensity, he thrust himself inside her. Pain blurred with pleasure as they were joined, entwined with each other. He stretched her until she was sure she'd break, but she submitted and gave herself to him. He was her king now, and she was whatever he needed her to be.

His muscular body drove her into the ground. Her neck was twisted as he gripped the leash tightly. He bit her, marking her with his passion and driving her to greater heights. She felt as much at the mercy of him as she had been at the storm, but this time, she knew she did not have to fear death. This time she had nothing to fear because the pleasure was too great.

Dazed and delirious, she gasped and moaned as her pleasure grew to bursting. He thundered into her, and she obediently erupted so much that her thighs became slick. With her cheek to the ground, she gazed at his perfect physique pounding into her and knew she was witnessing paradise.

She was brought back to reality as he pinned her down and used all his strength to dominate her. She was clamped to the floor by the leash in his one hand, while his other held her by her neck. She couldn't have moved from the harsh restraint even if she wanted to. All the while, the smile never left her face. Her need for more of what he offered remained insatiable.

The king took from her and gave to her in equal measure. No words were needed. He effortlessly read her response and knew she enjoyed his punishing pleasure, his animalistic lust and his control. Not a single word of either language was spoken between them, yet she felt a bond was forming. Her mind accepted his pleasure while her body was primed for him. She welcomed every part of him, from the tightness of the collar to the strength and hugeness of her king. Then it all flowed out of her, melting in one glorious cacophony of passion.

Her body was limp, her mind rendered mute and useless as everything had been drained from her. Yet, still he persisted. His stamina was strong until all the muscles in his body tensed, and he emptied himself inside her. As he did so, her eyes fluttered open. Her locket lay on the ground nearby; a sign of the society she had discarded.

She knew that she would never return. As far as anyone was concerned, she had died on that ship. Now, she had found her secret freedom.

Ashara Lightbringer ran through the forest so swiftly that the branches of nearby trees whipped her face. Her feet thudding into the ground, twigs cracked underneath the impact of her stride. She didn't have the opportunity to appreciate the beauty of the forest.

A golden sun shone in an azure sky, lush, verdant leaves hung from trees, and the whole world was vibrant with color. Ravens swooped across the sky, and Ashara wished she had the druidic ability to shift forms and take flight herself, but she was a simple bard who only knew basic magic.

There was only one way to get away from her pursuers, and that was to keep running and to get fortunate.

She slalomed through trees, her heart pounding in her chest and sweat trickling down her temples. Her purple hair flowed out behind her as she ran, and as she twisted her head back to catch a glimpse of her pursuers, her hair got caught in her mouth and she had to spit it out.

Ashara stumbled over a fallen log, but she did not lose her footing.

Behind her were Veran the barbarian and Christos the mage, two men who had been pursuing her for what seemed like an eternity, all for something as simple as information. She had almost lost them recently, but they had picked up her trail, thanks to a friend betraying her, and now she had to make it across the border to find allies who might house her. She could almost see the boundary in her mind, but it was still some way away.

She hoped to find a cave to hide in, but even that might not save her, given Veran's keen senses. Her only hope was that a wild animal might randomly appear and provide a distraction, but such a thing was at the whim of fate and not something to rely upon.

So, Ashara ran as quickly as her legs could carry her. And then, through the panic and the fear, she smiled.

***

In reality, Ashara Lightbringer wasn't Ashara Lightbringer at all, but Ashley Lawson, a girl in her mid-twenties who worked in a library and had always been fascinated by fantastical worlds and stories involving epic heroes and monstrous creatures. In real life, she was timid, uncertain, and rarely ventured out of her comfort zone. Everything in her life was regimented, and it was a life largely devoid of companionship and romance. They were foreign concepts to her, only existing in the realm of her imagination and between the pages of books. But when she played Dungeons & Dragons, the popular role-playing game, with her friends, she was able to break free of her shackles and become someone else—the person she had always wanted to be.

She had been attracted to Dungeons & Dragons from the first moment that she had played it. The act of playing another character was so freeing, allowing her to explore different aspects of her personality without taking any real risks. It was a safe space for her to let down the walls that she had erected that shut out other people, and she had made some good friends along the way.

Usually, the game was played around a table and involved pencils, paper, and a lot of dice rolling, but recently, Jonathan, their dungeon master, had heard of a group of people who were putting together a live action version of the game, and he had asked if anyone was interested. It had taken a lot of cajoling on the part of her party, but she had eventually agreed, figuring it wasn't really her taking part; it was Ashara, and Ashara was the type of person who always said yes to new experiences.

She had been upset at first, because there were far more people attending than she had realized, meaning she was split up from the people she knew. The game took place in the woods at the edge of the city. It helped the immersion to be so far away from everything she knew in her day-to-day life. She had always believed that she belonged in a different world, and now she could explore it in earnest.

It had taken some time to get used to the new way of playing. Instead of a strict set of rules that could be checked in a nearby rulebook, the game was administered by a group of wardens who roamed about the forest and followed various groups to ensure they were adhering to the few rules. It was much more of a free-form game than usual, and the freedom to do anything that was so alluring about the tabletop game was even more pronounced.

Ashley had fallen into the role of Ashara quickly and had thoroughly enjoyed the session so far. She had been given some information and been told that she wasn't to surrender it to Veran and Christos under any circumstances. She really felt the tension of what it would have been like to be on the run from desperate men, but it was only false tension. At the end of the day, she could return to her quiet life and be the prim, proper person she always was.

But she was determined to make her rendezvous and prove to herself that she could outwit the barbarian and the mage.

*

"STOP RUNNING, ASHARA. WE'RE COMING FOR YOU!" Veran shouted behind her.

She twisted her neck around and looked for them, but she saw nothing. However, she did end up barreling into a tree and felt a bloom of pain at her shoulder. She pressed herself against the wide trunk to try to catch her breath.

The only problem with being lost in the forest was that it was difficult to figure out where to go. She had been turned around a few times, and the longer the chase continued, the more likely it was that she would be captured. She tried to get her bearings, and then set off again.

She glanced down at her watch to check how long was left in the day before admonishing herself for doing so, because Ashara wouldn't have been able to do that and she wanted to make the experience as immersive and authentic as possible. As it turned out, there were still a good few hours left, so she didn't have to worry about the session ending too soon. She wanted to do something other than run, after all. She was even tempted by the idea of letting herself be caught. It was dangerous, but it offered a great opportunity for role-playing. It also sent a thrill slamming through her body. To be captured by two strong men made something tense inside her. She felt guilty for having such a dark fantasy but, in the end, it seemed all right, because it was happening to Ashara, not to Ashley. Even so, she wasn't going to give herself up so easily.

She thought about setting a trap for Veran and Christos, but unlike some other people, Ashley hadn't brought any resources with her. Because they were new, they hadn't realized that any equipment could be used if it was appropriate for the world that the wardens had created. It was a lesson for next time. Ashley almost couldn't wait for the next time, even though the first time had yet to be concluded.

Ashara, though, Ashara was scared. She fled through the bracken and was determined not to give up the secret that she held inside her mind. She had been entrusted with this information, and if she were to expose it, the rebellion might fell, for she knew the location of the rebel's camp.

A huge bounty had been placed on the rebel leader's head, which was why Veran and Christos were so adamant to capture and interrogate her. They were men driven by greed, and it was a matter of misfortune that Ashara had become a target.

Fear pulsed through her body as she sprinted away, assuming that she must be close to the safe boundary by now because she had been running for what seemed like forever.

She had been told that when she saw the Sunskull, she would be close. At first, she hadn't understood what a Sunskull was.

"You'll know it when you see it," was the only advice that she had been given, and at the time, it hadn't seemed enough. But then she saw a huge golden skull painted on a thick tree. It was indeed impossible to miss, and she smiled with relief.

Salvation was just moments away, and then the next part of her adventure would begin. She had already been thinking of what might happen. It seemed clear that she would join up with the rebellion and help them against the evil occupiers of the land. It was an epic tale, and Ashley couldn't wait to see how it was going to end.

She almost threw her arms up in triumph when she saw the Sunskull, which in game was the sign of the rebellion, but just as she was about to reach it, she heard a noise from behind her.

"I cast hold person!" Christos yelled.

"Ashara, STOP!" the warden replied.

Ashara's face twisted in agony as she realized that she had come so close. She could have flouted the rules and continued running, but that wasn't in the spirit of the game, and Ashley was too noble to do anything like that. So, she froze in place, acting like she had been bound by some magical force.

Dread tugged at her mind as the hunters closed in on her.

"Finally, we have you," Veran said, his words dripping with pride. He and Christos moved around to where Ashara could see them.

Ashara gulped with fear. She made an act of struggling against the spell, even though she knew it would have no effect.

"Ashara, Christos cast hold person, which means that, for the duration of the spell, you are unable to move. You can speak, and Christos can dispel the magic to free you if he chooses," the warden said.

Ashley nodded to show that she understood.

"You have something we want, Ashara. Now give it to us," Veran said.

"No," Ashara choked.

Veran strode up to her, wielding a thick wooden club. His mouth twisted into a wicked smile. His entire body bristled with strength.

He was being played by a man named Tom; a tall, broad-shouldered man who towered above Ashara. It was clear why he was playing a barbarian, because he was built for the role.

Ashley had always considered herself to be a refined girl who appreciated intellectual sophistication above everything else, but she couldn't deny the rumbling desire that crashed through her body like thunder when she saw such a prime specimen of a man standing before her.

He wore a loose vest that left his torso and biceps exposed, his taut skin glistening in the sun. Thick hair covered his chest and forearms, and his eyes were piercing sapphires.

Breath caught in her throat, and her heart pounded, almost afraid of her desire because she had never indulged anything like it before.

Even Christos was handsome—real name Christopher—although he was shorter than Veran and had a build that was more slender. He had his hands raised, and his fingers were bent as he held the spell.

"Talk, bard, or I'll pull you apart," Christos cackled.

"I'm not going to tell you anything," Ashara whimpered.

"Oh, I like a prisoner who struggles," Veran said.

Tom seemed to be a seasoned player of the game, as he had come prepared. The gnarled wood that made his club had been carved by him, and he wore fully appropriate gear. He had even painted two streaks down his right arm—one red and one blue—to symbolize his devotion to his people. He had a few feet of rope curled around his body as well, and a belt that had various different tools and pieces of equipment attached, as well as a waterskin.

Christos wore a blue robe—that was actually a bath robe—and had the emblem of a lightning bolt hanging around his neck, which was his magic symbol and was the artifact from which he drew his arcane power.

Veran closed the distance between them, and then walked behind her. Ashara caught his scent, and it played with her mind. It smelled so primal and earthy. It was such a raw, pure smell that caused chaos within her.

He shrugged the rope off his shoulder and unwound it from his body. Then he took a knife and cut the rope.

"You can release the spell now," he said as he took Ashara's arms and held them behind her body, pushing her voluptuous chest out. Her bodice was opened at the neck and offered a glimpse of her plunging cleavage, the dark valley between her breasts made of alluring shadows. It was almost as though her flesh was yearning to burst out.

She gasped as Veran took her hands and held her wrists together. He found it so easy to capture her tiny arms in his huge grip.

He wound the rope around her wrists then tied it in a tight knot. The rope bit into her skin.

Pain began to blur with pleasure. Ashley knew she shouldn't have been enjoying it, but the restraint made something bloom inside her, something foreign and taboo, something that she wanted more of. It was so vivid, in fact, that she wasn't entirely sure whether it was Ashara's desire or Ashley's, but she could not deny the sensations, and her cheeks flushed, ashamed that she was feeling this way because of strangers.

"I think we need to question you further. Let's take you somewhere more comfortable," Veran said. He took hold of her arm and dragged her along beside him.

Ashara could do nothing to resist. She had no magic that could help her and trying to escape Veran's grip wouldn't do any good because Christos would hit her with a magic spell immediately. She had to bide her time and wait for the right opportunity to present itself. Then she would try to escape. She knew that she was close to the Sunskull and thus to safety.

Thankfully, while they walked, they did not think to blindfold her, so she took great care to observe the surroundings and commit them to memory so that, if she escaped, she would be able to find her way back without too much trouble.

She also observed Veran. The brutish man handled her with such confidence and assertiveness. His hand encircled her entire arm, and he didn't let her go until they had reached their destination.

At the beginning of the day, they had been given a general layout of the area and told about some points of interest along the way, such as rivers and bridges, etc., but one of these points of interest was an old, squat barn, tucked away among some trees, the long branches tickling the roof. It had been the victim of a lightning strike at some point, as there was a huge gash in the roof and charred marks surrounding the point of impact. The door hung off one of the hinges, which creaked as Christos opened it, making way for Veran, Ashara, and the warden.

There was an old chair, which Christos pulled into the middle of the room. Then Tom pushed Ashara down and positioned her so that her arms were held behind her, helpless.

Surrounding her were bales of hay and old rusted farming equipment. There was a small rustling in the roof as a bird became disturbed by their entrance and went flying out of the hole in the roof.

They were alone.

"Now, bard, you can talk. I promise you that we're reasonable gentlemen and that you have nothing to fear from us ... as long as you tell us what we need to know," Veran said. He stood close by, while Christos kept his distance.

"I'll never talk. You won't ever get anything out of me," Ashara replied defiantly.

Veran cracked his knuckles. "I've made stronger people than you talk."

At that moment, the warden cleared his throat and stepped in, pulling the veil away from the world. "I just have to clarify that, if you are intending to go through with a torture scene, there are some ground rules. You cannot do anything physically harmful to another player, and if the player being tortured finds it too uncomfortable, things must come to an end immediately. Do you all understand?"

The three players nodded.

Ashara gulped again, and her eyes went wide with fear as Veran strode behind her.

"Now it's in your best interest to talk to us, bard; otherwise, my friend here will use more magic on you, magic that is more painful than the little spell he used before," Veran sneered.

"My name is Ashara."

"I don't care what your name is. You have information we need, and you're not leaving here alive unless we get it."

Ashara narrowed her eyes. "Then I suppose I'm not leaving here at all." She met Veran's gaze and saw an impressed twinkle in his eyes, a twinkle that she thought was more Tom than Veran.

"You're making this hard for us. You've made this hard for us already—getting us to chase you through the woods like some common rabbit. I want to get back and get my gold. I know there are few things bards value more than gold. After all, what else are you going to buy your fine clothes with? I can see you're in need of a new outfit, so here's what I'm going to do. I can offer you, say, fifty gold pieces for the information. That comes with a guarantee that your life will be spared."

Christos looked at him aghast. "You can't give away our reward. Not when we barely have enough to cover our expenses. We're in this to make money, not to pay rebels for their courtesy. The time to pay her was when we first encountered her, not now we have her tied up and at our mercy!" Christos said, apoplectic with rage.

Veran didn't even bother to look at the mage, his gaze focused entirely on Ashara.

"Is gold all that matters to you?" Ashara asked.

"It's the only thing that matters," Christos snapped.

"A bard with a heart of gold; a tale as old as time. You know you're helping a lost cause. The rebels aren't going to defeat the empire. The Sunskulls are going to be left cracked and broken, just like their country before them. It makes more sense to get gold while we can so we're prepared for the new world, and if civil war breaks out, then we have enough to get passage to safer lands," Veran said.

"If men like you stayed and fought, then maybe the rebels would stand a better chance of succeeding."

"And I'd stand a better chance of dying."

"I've never heard of a barbarian who was afraid of a little blood," Ashara said with disgust, spitting out her words so fiercely that bile flecked her lips.

Veran narrowed his eyes and widened his shoulders, leaning down so that his face was inches away from hers. "I fear nothing," he growled.

Ashley felt tingles spread all over her body, and she was left breathless. Her cheeks were flushed and her chest heaved. She had to remember that she was playing the role of a bard who had been captured by enemies, not as an innocent librarian who was tied to the chair, completely at the mercy of a sexy, strong, muscular barbarian.

She noticed how his gaze flicked down to her bosom, which made arousal prickle upon her flesh, for she had rarely been the object of desire for anyone. Heat spread all over her, and it felt as though she was being consumed by a fire.

"Then, why fear being a part of something bigger than yourself? Why not throw caution to the wind and fight for honor rather than gold?"

Before Veran could answer her question, Ashara heard frantic footsteps outside, and then the door to the barn burst open.

***

Standing before them was a panting man who was dripping with sweat.

"Warden, there's been an accident by the river. Marty slipped and hit his head. We're trying to pull him out, but he's out cold. Do any of you guys have a cell phone or know CPR?"

"I do," Christos said.

The warden glanced at Ashara then at the man who had just interrupted the interrogation. He licked his lips and looked uncertain for a moment before he clenched his jaw and made a decision. "Do you two think you can handle this scenario together? Tom, I know you're experienced; but Ashley, do you feel comfortable if I go and attend to this matter?"

"Of course. Go and see to Marty," Ashley said.

"Do you need any help?" Tom asked.

"No, I don't want to disrupt the game too much. We should be fine," the warden said, looking toward the panting man for confirmation.

"Just make sure you get the information out of her." Christopher winked as he left.

The whirlwind of people left the barn and, suddenly, Ashley was left alone with Tom.

***

As soon as the door closed behind them, they slipped back into their characters.

"I've fought for honor before. It doesn't put food on the table, and no cause is without sinners. The rebels might promise a better world, but they won't deliver. It's the same story over and over again. And, if you think this time is any different, then you're more naïve than I first thought."

"I'm not naïve. I just believe in something, in a cause that's greater than myself. You learn a lot being a bard, traveling from town to town, from inn to inn. You see how people really live, and nobody is happy under the emperor. The only way to get this country back to its feet is to stand up for what's right and help the people who are trying to make a difference in this world. The whole problem is that people just don't care any longer."

"Maybe they're right to. Kingdoms rise and fall," Veran said, holding his hand high in the air. "People always suffer. If you've been around all these different towns, then maybe you've seen the same things. You're a bard. You're supposed to shed light on the truth. So you really think it's worth throwing your life away?"

"Better than throwing my soul away. When it comes to the final judgment, I want to look back on my life and know that I did what was right. I want to feel proud of what I've done. I'm not going to sell out for some coin."

Veran snarled and clenched his fist. "I didn't want to hurt you," he said under his breath.

"Do your worst. I won't talk," Ashara said. "I came upon the information by accident. I hadn't thought of joining the rebellion before this. But now, seeing how people like you can be so easily swayed, I think they're desperate for people to help them. I'm going to join them, and I'm going to prove to you and everyone like you that you've made a mistake. And I'll tell everyone about the cowardly barbarian who preferred profit to war. I'll write a whole song about you—"

Veran's eyes blazed, and he shot out a hand, curling it around her throat. Ashara was silenced immediately and gagged. Her body went rigid with tension at the feeling of Veran's hand around her throat. There was something else that happened, as well. A deep twitch made incandescent flames burn inside her. It tore away all of her inhibitions and shot through her like a lance, leaving a sizzling trail.

Tom caught himself and, after a couple of moments, tore his hand away from her.

"I'm sorry," he said. "I got a little carried away."

"No," Ashley gasped. "It's okay. I ... I liked it. Let's play out the scene. I'll tell you if I want you to stop."

Red marks were around her throat, but in that moment, the mood had shifted, and suddenly, she realized she wasn't just playing a role-playing game any longer. Tom had been overwhelmed with a desire to do … things to her, things that were unspeakable normally. She found herself longing to be at his mercy, to feel his touch again, to do all the things that she had read about in books, to experience all the wild, tormented fantasies that had careened through her mind; the fantasies that she had been afraid to look at for they had burned brighter than the sun.

A lifetime had been spent hiding away from her true desires, because she had wanted to lock herself away in a room and run from these taboo thoughts, but now, here with him, she felt safe expressing them, because it wasn't really her; it was Ashara.

Tom snarled once again. "Maybe if I have a little fun with you, I'll make you talk and you'll eventually beg for mercy."

"I'll never beg!" she yelled then spat at his feet, wanting to make him angry again, wanting to enrage him.

His cheeks flushed, and his huge body bristled with anger. Her bosom heaved, and sweat trickled down the middle of her chest, settling into the valley of her cleavage. There was added danger, as she knew that, at any moment, someone could come bursting through the door.

Tom had his hands on her again, around her neck, clamped tightly to her flesh. He then spread his huge hand across her chest and dropped down. He could have all of her if he wanted. He could take her, and there was absolutely nothing she could do about it.

He started to slowly pull away the lace that was holding her bodice together. With every strap that loosened, Ashley gasped.

Breath caught in her throat, and her heart beat so forcefully she was sure it was going to burst clean through her chest.

Her lips parted. Her body ached for him. The power he displayed was so primal and raw that it was irresistible. Her mind grew hazy, as though she had been intoxicated by some enchantment, but the only spell was one of lust, which played havoc with her mind.

Tom looked at her directly, and she met his gaze as he slipped his hand into the loosened bodice and groped her breast.

As he swept his fingers along the rise of her bosom, her sensitive nipple hardened, and she whimpered in mercy. Tom smirked and did it again, teasing and torturing her before he opened her bodice completely and let her breasts pour through. He grunted and growled as he saw her voluptuous curves and placed his hands upon them, squeezing and caressing them before he leaned down and licked her nipples then nibbled on them, sending jolting shots of pleasure through her body.

His grip suddenly turned stronger as he started to feel his way around the rest of her body. He ran his hands down the middle of her belly then down her thighs, his biceps tensed and every part of him crying out for the attention of a woman.

Ashley let her mouth hang open. Her head lolled to the side as he rose again, keeping one hand on her warm breast before he started to undress, letting the rope fall to the floor, dropping his vest and tunic, revealing every inch of his barbarian, masculine prowess. His body was sculpted in angular muscles, prime and ready for war. He was a warrior, and Ashley flushed with desire.

"By the gods …" she gasped as her gaze dropped to his erection, which was long, hard, and ardent with desire. Rippling veins ran like rivers under his taut flesh, and the smooth, mushroom tip teased and taunted her. She swallowed a lump in her throat as he came up to her and grabbed a fistful of her hair.

"Bards are always known for their sweet mouths. Let's see how sweet yours is," he growled as he gripped her head and smeared his cock over her cheeks, finding her mouth.

She felt the heat spread over her face until it was inside her, between her lips. She wrapped them tightly around him and flicked her gaze up to meet his eyes.

Veran brought her head back and forth, using her mouth the way he wanted, as she was helpless to struggle against him. She loved it.

She gagged and groaned as he slammed into her mouth, making her take him as deeply as she could go until she felt it hit the back of her throat. Her eyes fluttered shut, overwhelmed by the feeling of pleasuring him, knowing that he was this aroused because she was at his mercy, tied up and ready to be used.

Fire burned in her soul, a fire so powerful that she thought she might pass out at one point, such was the force of the passion. All the books she had read, all the fantasies she had imagined hadn't been anything compared to this. It was raw and furious and wrong, and yet it felt so right. It was the most wonderful, serene sensation she had ever felt. It burned away all the hypocrisy of the world and was the only thing that made sense.

Her head was jerked from up and down as Veran fucked her face. Soon enough, his erection was coated with saliva. It dripped from him and from her mouth, foamy and wet. She was groggy.

When he took his erection away, she tried to move toward it, wanting more. It was never enough. She wanted to gorge on him forever and had so quickly become addicted to his erection that it was painful to not have it touching her or inside her. Her mouth was raw and aching, but she whimpered for him, although she was silenced by his kiss.

Then he pulled down her pants and revealed her wet pussy. She was already soaking from how turned on she was at being tied up. It ran down her thighs as Veran bent down.

"Smells sweet," he grunted before digging his fingers into her thighs and starting to tease her, bringing his hands so close to her pussy then pressing down on it before taking them away.

It grew hot and cold, and then, suddenly, his lips were on hers again, kissing her so firmly that she was sure bruises were going to appear on her lips. The thought that he would mark her so fiercely with his passion was more of a turn on, so much so that she actually started to shake in the chair.

He toyed with her, plunging his finger into her, curling it back and forth slowly, before ramming it in and making her tremble with ecstasy. He somehow seemed to know exactly what to do, exactly what she needed to take her to the brink of pleasure, but he always stopped before she collapsed fully, denying her these orgasms, driving her insane and wild with these dark cravings.

"Tell me what you know!" he yelled.

Ashley bit her lower lip and shook her head vehemently, only to then whimper as he pulled out his wet fingers again and slid them across her lips so she was forced to taste herself.

In this instance, Ashara would have broken—there was no doubt about that—but Ashley refused, because she knew, if she did, it would be over. She wasn't ready for it to end yet. She wanted more. A monster had been unleashed inside her, and she wouldn't be satisfied until it had been fed.

Veran returned to playing with her. He had one hand against her pussy, the other fondling her breasts, grabbing her hair, and clamping over her mouth to play with her breath.

Her skin burned. She was so close to that sweet climax. It had been building inside her so fervently that she was sure, when it came, it was going to erupt like a volcano and her scream was going to be as loud as a banshee. She was just a toy for the barbarian.

She felt him play with her, his fingers working their magic. This time, she knew he wasn't going to torture her. This time, it was going to be what she wanted. What she needed.

She closed her eyes and saw a bright light ahead of her. Was it heaven? If this was death, then it was the way she wanted to go.

A blazing fury seized her body in rapture, and the pleasure hit her like a thunderstorm. It made her entire body crackle with electricity, and she swore she saw lightning before her eyes. Her scream would have been loud, but it was muffled by Veran's strong hand. She struggled to breathe, and this only added to the sensation.

She was still reeling from the messy, wrecking ball of a climax when Tom stood before her and picked up the rope. He whipped her with the thick end, the cord leaving huge, red marks against her flawless, supple pale skin. Each one brought with it a squeal of pleasure, and the pain shimmered across her body. She was too weak to do anything about it. All she wanted was to be fucked. To have the life fucked out of her.

Veran was still as hard as a rock when he threw the rope away and plunged himself inside her, overwhelming her with his strength. Her body arched as he slid inside her. She was wet and tight, and he groaned and shuddered as he felt her take him.

He clamped his hands around her neck again, and they stared at each other while he fucked her. Ashley gazed in his eyes and saw the raw, unbridled energy. It was the most beautiful thing she had ever seen. He was as captivated by these feelings as she was. They were sharing something intimate, something unspoken, something that was going to stay in this barn.

Ashley groaned loudly as Tom shuddered. She could feel him getting stronger and stronger. She was afraid that she wouldn't be able to handle it, that her body was going to be torn apart.

Some part of her wanted that fate.

Tom unleashed all his energy on her, and it came in a blitz of a supernova. Her clothes had been pulled all over the place. There were hand marks on her body, and his sweat had dripped and drizzled on her skin, sizzling as it splashed against the burning flesh.

His almighty roar was bestial and made her stomach flutter. She felt the warm explosion as she was almost torn from the chair.

Tom slumped against her when it was over. They were both breathless.

Ashley's mind collapsed in on itself as she tried to process what had just happened. It had all been so quick and so wonderful, but how could she do this in her real life?

In that moment, she didn't really care. All that mattered was that it had happened. For the first time in her life, she felt as though she was really and truly alive rather than just playing at life.

Tom staggered back, almost as much in shock as she had been. "So, where do we go from here?" he asked.

She wasn't sure if it was Veran or Tom asking, and she didn't know if Ashley or Ashara would answer.

"Come on Mom, what else are you going to do on New Year's Eve?" Mandy asked, a pleading look in her eyes.

Diana sighed and looked over at her daughter, who was taller and had more striking features. Mandy had taken after her father. She was a beautiful girl. Diana was approaching fifty, still with the womanly curves that had been passed down from generation to generation. She had long tawny brown hair that reached the small of her back, soft full lips, and a sense that the best years of her life were behind her.

"I thought I would have a quiet night this year. I can watch fireworks on TV, and I might just have some me time, you know, finish a book, maybe do a jigsaw puzzle…"

"Mom," Mandy crossed her arms, "you're not retired, and you still have plenty of life in you. I'm not going to stand here and watch you fade away."

"I hardly think reading a book means I'm fading away."

"You know what I mean," Mandy's tone turned from annoyance to concern. "I know this year has been difficult for you, but you can't just let life slip by. I've always loved your spirit, and it just makes me sad that you seem so ready to give up on everything. You're not doing anything with your friends, and I'd just feel horrible if I was out there having fun and knew that you were back here by yourself, dwelling and moping until midnight approaches."

"There's nothing wrong with spending some time by myself," Diana said defensively, "and I'm not going to be moping. I'll just reflect and prepare myself for a new year."

"And think of Dad?" Mandy arched an eyebrow. "I'm only back for a few more weeks. I want to know that you're okay. I hate thinking of you being alone."

"You don't have to worry about me, Mandy. I'm not a child. I know how to take care of myself, and I'm perfectly fine being alone. If your father got bored and wanted to go off and have a fling with a girl just about young enough to be his granddaughter, then that's fine, he can have his little fun. It's no skin off my nose. And I don't want you to be worried about me. You go and have fun. It'll be nice for you to see Jack again. I always liked him. He would have been a good match for you."

"Don't try to change the subject." Mandy rolled her eyes. "You know Jack and I have only been friends, and that's all we will ever be. You should come Mom."

"Do you really think I'm going to fit in with you and your friends? I remember a time when the very thought of me coming to one of your parties would have filled you with horror."

"Yeah, well, I was wrong to think that," Mandy conceded, "and this will make up for all my difficult years. It's not like we're teenagers anymore. This isn't going to be a party filled with drugs and alcohol. It's going to be a sophisticated affair. Remember that Jack is a writer; he has a different way about him now."

Diana sensed that it was going to be more trouble to keep arguing with Mandy than to simply surrender and agree to go to the party.

It might not be such a bad thing, she thought, *and it will probably be better than spending the night by myself.* There was a time when she never had a shortage of parties to go to on New Year's Eve, but over time, the vigor in her social life had diminished—helped, in part, by her divorce.

The raw pain was over now, but a numb emptiness remained where there had once been love. Mostly, it had been a mutual affair, although David had been the one to put forward the idea. Neither of them had been happy for a long time. Once Mandy had grown old enough to have a life of her own, Diana and David hadn't had all that much in common any longer. The realization had been sad and difficult, but in the end, it was the only way either of them could move forward.

Passion and excitement had long been missing from Diana's life. Memories of those two emotions were just a whispered echo. David had easily found a way to bounce back and give himself a jolt of energy, while she was still searching for what she needed. It was annoying.

"Who knows, you might meet someone," Mandy added.

Diana pressed her lips together. Those chances were slim. She'd been on a few dates, but none of them provided her with any sort of spark. The men she'd met all seemed to be at a stage of life where they were settled in their ways and had no sense of discovery. Heartbroken, they wanted companionship more than love, but she'd had that. She wanted to go back in time and experience the thrill of a new romance; the lust and yearning that came with the unknown. Life was a series of shifting scenes and landscapes, and the expectations seemed to change as she moved through each one. Diana wasn't ready to give up, though. She wasn't sure what she was looking for or where she was going to find it, but she wanted to give herself the chance that she might find something to make her smile again.

"I'm not sure about that, but I suppose it might be a good idea to get the year started off in the right spirit. It will be good to see Jack again. I haven't seen him for a long time," Diana admitted.

"You won't regret it!" Diana said, hugging her mother. "I'll call Jack now and tell him to expect one more. It'll be a great birthday surprise for him."

***

A few days passed before it was time for the party. Christmas had been a very calm period for which Diana was grateful. It was an improvement from the previous year. Mandy came back for her usual visit, and it had been a whirlwind. Diana and David had promised to make a concerted effort to rekindle their love and affection for each other. One month into their mutual resolution, David failed miserably. His affair came to light, and there was really no way forward for the two of them. Diana had spent the better part of the year dealing with all the paperwork and getting used to being on her own again. For so long, she had been in a partnership. Now, she had to walk the path by herself. The future—a bleak, grey landscape—robbed her of any ideas about how to get back to a good point in her life.

While Mandy was there, Diana put on a brave face and didn't let on to how forlorn she felt. Mandy lived her own life abroad with a successful job and a happy life. Diana wanted to make sure that Mandy had a happy time and didn't have a vacation that was filled with misery and grim depression. But the spring of Mandy's visit would fade in a wintry darkness when Diana was left alone again. She would look around at the shadows that surrounded her and sigh.

For the time being, though, she had Mandy. The two went out shopping, for lunch, and just spent time together watching movies and TV. Spending time with her daughter was so nice, but it was bittersweet because it would be over so quickly.

"I wish you could stay longer," Diana said.

"Me too, Mom. It would be nice if every day could be like these days, but then I guess maybe we wouldn't appreciate it as much."

"No, you'd probably be screaming at me like you did when you were seventeen."

"I wouldn't have had to scream if you would have let me go out when I wanted," Mandy retorted, teasing her mother with a smile.

"There was no way I was going to let you go to all the places you wanted to go, like that beach party where everyone was far older than you."

"Oh, you know nothing would have happened to me. Jack would have looked after me."

"He always did," Diana said, smiling softly. "I need to thank him for that. So, do you think there's going to be any magic this new year?"

"I don't know. Maybe. There is someone at work…we've been flirting a little bit. I don't know if it's going to go anywhere, though. We're all so busy, it's hard to find the time."

"You have to find the time for the important things. I know it's not always easy, but if you don't, then you'll end up wondering what you worked so hard for," Diana said in a motherly tone. "Unfortunately, it's too easy to let things get in the way. It's about time you had some light in your life."

Mandy could have said the same thing about her mother.

***

Diana wasn't sure what to wear for the party. Being a special occasion and so long since she had dressed up, she chose a red, velvety dress that clung to her curves and had a plunging neckline. She wore a slender gold necklace and some dangling earrings which sparkled. When Mandy saw her, she was astonished. Diana accentuated her natural beauty with a touch of makeup. The transformation was amazing. Dressing up made her feel young and excited. Now, she felt foolish over resisting Mandy's efforts to get her to come to this party.

Of course, Diana felt as though her own efforts paled in comparison to Mandy. Diana's daughter could capture everyone's attention just by entering a room. She had a bombshell figure and dark, haunting features. It was a wonder that she hadn't been snapped up by a good man. Diana wondered if there wasn't some latent anguish about her daughter not pursuing Jack. The two had always had such a good rapport. Diana had been convinced that their relationship ran deeper. Both had always denied it, though. Still, Diana wouldn't be surprised if something happened between them at the party.

***

They arrived at Jack's large house. Diana was surprised at the sight of so many glittering cars and people. The house was massive, with a towering roof and every window winking at them with a bright shining light. Vines crept up the walls, and there was a welcoming fountain outside.

"He's certainly done alright for himself," Diana remarked.

"Yes, his hard work has paid off. It seems like only yesterday that we were sitting in his Mom's basement talking about all his wild ideas. They seemed crazy at the time. I always wondered if anybody would find them as fascinating as I did."

"I guess they did," Diana said.

They moved inside and the chattering noise rose around them, as though they were being plunged into water. Diana made sure to stick close to Mandy, as she was in danger of getting lost in this throng. The house teemed with people of all ages. Diana gazed in wonder at the wide spaces and the ornaments on display. The man who owned this was the same man she had cooked for when he'd come over for dinner.

Everyone seemed to be in good spirits. The catering staff were on hand to ply everyone with drinks. A glass of sparkling wine, sweet and bubbly, was thrust into Diana's hand. It certainly did a lot to take the edge off the moment. Mandy led her by the hand through the house until they found Jack, who was in the middle of a crowd entertaining some people with a story. Diana's jaw dropped when she saw him.

She could barely believe it was the same boy she had welcomed into her home. A *man* stood before her; all masculine strength and vigor. He radiated sheer power with a magnetic aura that drew in everyone.

Diana's skin prickled when his piercing gaze fell on her. He had strong cheekbones and broad shoulders. His silk shirt was open at the collar, with dark hair emerging from the opening. His waist was trim, and his sleeves were rolled up to the middle of his forearm. He had a lazy smile, but he looked delighted when he caught sight of Mandy and Diana.

Immediately, he excused himself from his current conversation and rushed over to them. He hugged Mandy excitedly, wrapping his arms around the small of her back and lifting her off her feet. Diana didn't get the same reception. Instead, he kissed her lightly on the cheek. She caught the scent of his musky aftershave, and her mind grew hazy with desire. Her breath caught in her throat, and her heart raced. How could it be that this was the same Jack she had known in his youth?

The simple answer was that this *wasn't* the same Jack. He had grown and matured into a handsome man. His once awkward body had filled out into a muscular epitome of manliness. He had an easy, relaxed confidence about him that was intoxicating.

"Mrs. Vance, it's so good to see you again. You haven't changed at all; you're still as beautiful as ever," he said. Diana blushed.

"Actually, it's just Diana, Jack, I'm not a 'Mrs.' anymore," she said, raising her hand to show her bare finger where once her wedding ring had rested. Jack's face fell.

"I'm so sorry, Diana. Now, I remember Mandy mentioning something about that. I'm always putting my foot in it," Jack apologized.

"It's okay," Mandy said, "She's here to start the new year off with a bang, so if you know of any eligible bachelors, please send them her way."

"I'll keep that in mind," Jack said, although his gaze drifted over Diana again in a strange way; if she hadn't know him better, she might think that he was checking her out. He was young enough to be her son, and he was her daughter's best friend. She shook her head and told herself to stop being an old fool. Things didn't magically happen like that.

"Congratulations on your book. It's good to know that sometimes good things can happen to good people," Diana said.

"Thank you so much," Jack pressed his hand to his heart. "Did you read it?"

"I'm afraid that things with dragons aren't really in my wheelhouse."

"Oh, well, nobody's perfect," Jack chuckled, "but I can still hook you up with a signed copy if you'd like one." He leaned in and narrowed his voice, covering his mouth with his palm to shield his words from the rest of the room and forming an intimate moment between the two of them. His breath was sweet and slightly tinged with the scent of alcohol. "Just keeping it between you and me, I don't want to be signing books all night. I don't think my hand can take it."

Diana giggled and then Jack was called away by someone else who wanted to revere in his presence. Jack promised

Diana and Mandy that he would return soon enough. Diana was left biting her lower lip, watching this magnificent specimen of a man walk away. She let these forbidden and tempting thoughts run through her mind before she resigned herself to the fact that she was just a mature woman while Jack was just being polite and charming.

Mandy saw a few people she recognized. She was unwilling to leave Diana, but Diana told her to go have fun. Diana would have to get used to doing things by herself anyway. She clutched her glass of wine and started to wander around the house. There were large rooms that were more like hallways. One of the staircases was roped away and there were a lot of people milling about. From the errant conversation, Diana came to understand that the staircase led to Jack's basement office where he worked his magic and came up with his stories; a place in which no intruder was allowed. This of course created some mystique around the room and plenty of people offered suggestions about what could be hidden down there. Some of the notions were entirely fanciful, and Diana moved away from them swiftly as she didn't want to get caught up in any idle speculation.

She ended up in conversation with a few people as the night wore on, although none of them made as much of an impression as Jack had. It felt so wrong to be so taken with Jack, but she couldn't get him off her mind. Diana caught glimpses of him through the night and ran after him, as though she was a star chasing the sun, but he was elusive and seemed to disappear every time she thought she was close. Mandy came back to Diana time and time again, each time a little more intoxicated than the last. She was having fun, and Diana had to lie to her and say that she was having fun, too.

While it was good to be out of the house and spending time around people, Diana was left with a feeling that she didn't quite belong. She was an outsider, an observer. The world seemed to rotate around her at a blistering pace, and she couldn't quite find the right moment in which to step. She was disoriented, and it soon became quite clear that there wasn't any place for her. It was as though she had been left behind completely. This time last year she had been a married woman. She had had an identity. She knew where she stood, who she was, but now she had to relearn all that, and she wasn't entirely sure how.

"You don't look like you're having fun," Jack asked her. Diana gasped, startled by his sudden appearance. She had backed away into a corner, receding into the silence while the party raged on without her, expecting that nobody would miss her presence. People were filtering outside, getting ready for the final countdown to usher in the New Year and Diana was being left behind. But Jack had somehow found her.

"I…I'm just not used to being at parties by myself I guess."

"You're not by yourself, I'm here," Jack said, smiling warmly. Diana returned the gesture. She could feel his gaze upon her, and it burned, filling her with warmth. She looked away from him, feeling self-conscious and uneasy.

"I really am sorry about what happened before. I hope I didn't offend you."

"It's okay Jack, really, I didn't think anything of it."

"What happened, if you don't mind me asking? You and Mr. Vance always seemed pretty good together, at least as far as I can remember."

"We were, back then, but a lot of things change," Diana smiled as she gestured to the house. Jack looked sheepish. "It's just the standard story of people getting bored with each other, I think. We both wanted something new and we couldn't find it in each other, so we decided to look elsewhere. He just happened to find it before I did." When Jack gave her a quizzical look, Diana explained about the affair her ex-husband had had.

Jack scowled in disgust. "That's the lowest of the low. You know, if you like, I can base a character off him in my next book and get him eaten by some vicious monster?"

This made Diana laugh. "I'll think about it. If you do, I might have to read that one. That's enough about me and my troubles anyway. Tell me about yourself. What lucky lady has managed to capture your heart?"

"Oh, actually there isn't anyone. I've been too busy working to even think about a relationship. There are too many words that need to be written, and now I have too many characters in my heart to make room for someone else."

"Now, that sounds like the kind of answer you'd give at an interview," Diana pursed her lips and gave him a challenging look. Jack held out his hands, as if to say, 'you got me'. Diana couldn't believe that someone like him was single. He had it all; money, looks, house, talent. He was quite a catch.

"Can I ask you a question Jack?" she asked.

"Of course."

"I hope you won't think I'm a meddling mother, but there's something I've always been wondering about you and Mandy…why did you never get together? You've always been so well-suited, and you've always gotten on well. Sometimes I was even jealous of you two because you had the kind of rapport that I wanted with my husband. I know you have both always insisted that you were nothing but friends, but has there never been anything more? Not even a hint?"

"I really…I'm not sure I should be talking about this. I don't know if Mandy would like it."

"It'll be our little secret. I promise, I won't say anything."

Jack took a breath and looked at the people wandering outside. Some of them called out to him, and he replied that he would be out in just a moment.

"A long time ago there was maybe a hint of something happening. You know, we've been close our whole lives and, when we were teenagers, it was a crazy time. But it never happened. There was a time when I thought I might be in love with her, and I think a little later there was a time when she thought she was in love with me, but we both decided that ultimately it was better to stay as friends. You know, she wanted to go off and live life and see the world. I wanted to stay here and write my stories. Even if there was anything, it was never going to work."

"That's such a shame. If I had known…I would have done anything for you two to be happy. Maybe I could talk to her. Maybe I could convince her to stay another few weeks…"

Jack laughed. "You don't have to worry, Diana. We're both happy and I don't have any regrets with the way my life has turned out. I'm exactly where I want to be, and to be honest, even though Mandy means a lot to me, she's always been the exception to the rule. She's not exactly my type."

Diana looked aghast. "Not your type? What on earth do you mean? I know I'm biased because I'm her mother but come on, she's gorgeous! How could she not be your type?" Diana paused then as realization dawned upon her face. "Oh, wait, I get it…you prefer men."

Jack laughed warmly and stepped closer towards Diana, engulfing her in his presence. "No Diana, not men. I just prefer my women to be a little more…mature."

As the words left his lips, his eyes gleamed with desire and Diana suddenly realized that she hadn't been mistaken at all. He really had been looking at her purposefully.

"Can I make a confession?" he asked. Diana nodded, for she was speechless. "When I was younger, it wasn't Mandy I fantasized about…it was you. I could barely control myself around you, and you're just as sexy now as you were then." His words rushed out in warm breath, and his hand slipped around her waist. Diana could barely believe it was happening, but she didn't want it to stop. Yet, it seemed so illicit and taboo. She glanced around in fear.

"Let's go somewhere more private," Jack suggested, as though he was reading her mind. He took her hand and led her down towards his basement. He unclipped the rope and then opened the doors, ushering her in and closing them behind him so that they were all alone.

He turned on the light, and Diana was stunned. In one corner was the computer where he wrote, but the room was dominated by a bed and all manner of paraphernalia on the wall. Whips and floggers hung down alongside collars and handcuffs, most of them black leather. There were other things that she couldn't even begin to describe. The bed was wide and long, with posts rising from the corners that had space for handcuffs.

"What is this place?" she whispered.

Jack walked up behind her. He towered above her. He was half her age, but he felt twice as huge. His hands rested on her hips, and they felt as though they always belonged there. The warmth of his body pressed against her, and she closed her eyes. Arousal surged through her blood, making it feel hot.

"This is where I write, where I feel most comfortable. This is my whole world," he said, "and I don't bring many people back here. Only the ones I can trust."

"Why do you think you can trust me?" Diana asked, still unable to open her eyes.

"Because I know what you need. I know what you've been waiting for. It wasn't right when I was younger. I still had a lot to learn. I had a lot of growing up to do. But now I'm here. I saw it in your eyes tonight. I can feel it in your body now. There's something inside you just yearning to break free. You've been waiting for the right person to unlock the secrets inside you, the desire you've been so afraid to face."

"I…" she began but couldn't finish the thought.

"You probably don't even know what it is you need, but I do. You need to let go."

As he said this, he raised his hand and brought it around her neck, his fingers curling over her skin, placing pressure on her throat. It made her gasp, although it wasn't enough to threaten her life. But the pain, the strength, the force with which he handled her was enough to make her weak at the knees. Her mind rippled with the pleasure of submission and went to wild places. Never had anyone treated her with such strength and confidence. Never had anyone told her so plainly what he wanted, and she loved the feeling of being the object of someone's desire, especially when the flame had been kindled over years and it had grown to a simmering intensity.

"How are you doing this?" Diana asked. She gave herself to his strength and leaned back into him, trusting that he would take hold of her and never let her go.

"A long time ago, I learned to go after what I wanted and never be afraid to indulge my desires. There are too many ways we miss out on everything important in life. I've developed an instinct, and I can see it in others, too. I saw it in you; a troubled soul who needs some guidance. In this room I shed all the costumes I must wear in the outside world. There," he pointed to the typewriter, "is where I lay my soul bare, and here," he moved his hand to the bed, "is where I lay my body and indulge everything primal and savage. I struggled with the two sides of myself for a long time, but in order to do my best work there," Again, he pointed to the desk, "I must be a beast. Diana, it's almost a new year. What kind of woman are you going to be? Do you want to hide from yourself, or do you want me to show you who you really are?"

"Show me, Jack, God, show me!" He turned her around, and she gazed into his eyes. They could hear the faint chorus of the crowd counting down the end of the year, but it all faded away as Diana felt herself melting into him. He mouthed the numbers, and with each one they were pulled inexorably closer to each other. It was as though they were being pulled together by a force of nature, but she knew it wasn't nature at all. It was him.

3…

She could feel the breath on her lips.

2…

Her eyes closed as his hands ran around the small of her back and squeezed tightly.

1…

Their breath swirled together as their lips met, and a dormant desire rose through Diana's body. She wrapped her arms around his neck and felt the heat emanating from his younger, powerful body. She wanted this, needed it, desired everything he'd promised most of all. Their tongues danced and her mind exploded in kaleidoscopic delight. Fireworks exploded outside, but they were nothing compared to the passion that exploded within her.

Diana's entire body pulsated and throbbed with a craving and, as she and Jack broke apart, she saw the same desire reflected in his eyes. His hands roamed all around her body, turning her around again as though she were just a toy. She closed her eyes and let him feel her, loving the way his hands roamed over the curves of her body and squeezed, teasing every inch of her. A sensual smile played upon her lips as his hand came up over her breasts and rested on the top of her chest, before it went further and curled around her neck once more. His other hand felt the curve around her hips and then made the short journey up her back. His huge palms and long fingers made short work of the space, and she felt him tugging at her zipper.

"Wait," she said, twisting her neck to look at him. Shame flowed through her. She wasn't as young as she used to be. Far from her prime, she was even far from the woman she had been when Jack was a teenager.

"Your body is mine now," he said in a low voice, "and I want to enjoy everything you have to offer."

He pushed her towards the bed roughly and yanked the zipper down. Her head slammed against the mattress and her hair splayed out all around her. His hands gripped her hips and pulled her closer to him. She could feel his arousal, hard and ardent, bigger than she ever remembered it being with her husband. She groaned as he peeled away her dress and threw it aside, and then turned her around. Her legs arched up and her arms were by her side. His hand dragged down along the middle of her body, over her breasts, down her stomach, brushing against her thighs. She writhed as she watched his fingers dig into her flesh, and she groaned loudly, moaning with desire. Her body cried out to him to take her.

She lost all pretense of doubt. It didn't matter that Jack was her daughter's childhood best friend. Jack was a changed man from the quiet teenager she remembered. He throbbed with confidence and experience. In a way, she felt like the younger one. He was sexually powerful, and she wanted him to show her everything he promised.

His hands ran down her thighs, parting her legs. She writhed and whimpered, reaching out to his body, feeling his strong hands and forearms. He pulled her bra and her panties off, tossing them away.

"You're so fucking sexy," he said as he began to undress, unbuttoning his shirt, unclasping his belt, until he had exposed every inch of himself to her. How she loved it. Oh, she moaned loudly, and her mouth started to drool when she saw his younger body in front of her; the thick throbbing erection that promised so much pleasure. She was completely at his mercy, and she loved it. All she wanted was to be used by him and to let go.

Jack smirked as he started to play with her, teasing her with his dancing fingers. He brought the soaking tips up and down her thighs, leaving glistening streaks of warm wetness. Fervent gasps rippled out of her as sweat began to prickle on her exposed flesh. Jack loomed over her, a god who was baptizing her in fire. His fingers worked furiously inside her and reached into the deepest part of her, making her soul tingle.

As he touched her, she realized that he was right; she needed this more than ever. For too long now, she had forgotten who she was. Perhaps, she had never truly realized. Her husband hadn't been the right partner for her, and all she'd had to do was wait for the right man to mature into a confident, dominant man. One who could take her body into his hands and mold her like putty. One who could control her sensations and cause a whirl of delight to swirl around her mind.

Orgasmic energy raged within her like a maelstrom, making every part of her bubble and boil. It had all been locked inside her, and Jack had held the key. It all flooded out in one long, seemingly unending flow of slick, syrupy delight. Her body tingled and shuddered as it came out. Jack moved along her body, fondling her breasts, and then suddenly she felt hard heat in her mouth as he cupped her head and guided her warm, willing lips to make love to him, which she did so eagerly. She murmured with delight as she took him in her mouth and swirled her tongue around his shaft, feeling the rippling veins along the taut skin. His long arms reached down and continued to play with her. Diana watched as he brought his fingers up and then slid them into his mouth, sucking on them deeply and eagerly.

Jack brushed strands of hair away from her face, resting his hand on her scalp as he groaned. She couldn't believe how turned on she was getting at being played with by a younger man, and the only thought running through her mind was that she didn't want this to be the only time. She wanted, *needed* more, and Jack was so attuned to her desires that he could practically read her mind. He pulled her head away and moved back down her body. Jack took hold of his erection and smeared it across her thighs. She felt the burning heat scorch her and the aching intensity grew to almost unbearable levels. It was only taken away when he thrust inside her, and a whole new world of delight was shown to her. A guttural howl escaped her lips as his arm clamped around her neck and held her in place. He became the beast he'd promised. He snarled and grunted, and his body erupted in flames, at least it felt that way to Diana.

She let go, just as he had commanded. Finally, she was free to be herself. She had found her place, and it was being at Jack's mercy.

Lucia's body prickled with sweat as the sun beat down on her olive skin. Her shoulders were slumped, and her hands were in shackles. She shuffled along the sandy path, linked together with other woman by a thick rope hanging between their necks in a long line. There must have been at least fifty of them. She had been taken in a raid from her home by the Pharaoh's men.

The Pharaoh was ruthless. Every small tribe and village lived in fear of his soldiers coming to them, for they left nothing but dust and blood in their wake. Lucia was young, but on this day, she felt old. She had seen devastation and death, and she had been torn from her home.

Some guards walked beside her and looked upon the women with hunger. She felt their eyes roam about her body, gazing at her supple olive skin and her curves . were covered by thin white cloth. Lucia tried not to look at them, for she was afraid what would happen to her if she did, She caught the eye of one who came up to her and placed his hand upon her arm. She tried to wrench it away, but he was too strong. His grip only tightened, as he snarled at her with a row of straight teeth. Nothing but cruelty rested in his eyes, spiking fear within her.

"Leave her. She is Pharaoh's. Until he has made his judgment, all these women are his. But afterwards, we will get our share," another guard said.

The one holding her took a moment to release her. When he took his arm away, he licked his lips. Lucia knew that, if the Pharaoh didn't choose her, she would be left at the mercy of this guard. She did not like the thought of that at all.

Her head hung down, and she wished that some beast from the sky would fly down and pluck her away, for death seemed the only release from her dark fate. Ever since his wife had died, the Pharaoh had been searching the country for someone to pleasure him and worship him. He had sent his men out far and wide to bring women to his side in the hope that one of them would be worthy of him.

As yet, none had been. Lucia certainly didn't think that she would be the one to find his favor. The other women were each prettier than the last. She couldn't stop herself from wondering what kind of man the Pharaoh was that he was so unimpressed with such beauty that was offered to him. She'd heard the stories as well. The women he didn't choose were given to his guards as a reward for their loyalty and hard work. Some of them returned to the village while others were never heard from again. Those that did return were ravaged and raw and, more often than not, with child.

Lucia knew that she would never return home. She could not bear the shame, but she did not want to be at the mercy of the Pharaoh or his guards, either. Both were as bad as each other. She had not met the Pharaoh personally, of course, but stories of his cruelty and strength traveled across the land. He was imbued with the power of a god. He led his people with a respect born out of fear. Lucia was almost afraid of even thinking anything bad about the Pharaoh, as she was afraid that he would somehow know what was in her heart. He was a god, after all. There was no telling the limit to his powers.

In some ways, she knew it was her duty to serve her Pharaoh. Yet, in her heart, she longed for a simple life. She knew she would never compare with these other woman. A life passed around by his guards seemed to be the only fate left to her. That made her heart sink.

She looked at the footprints left behind in the soft golden sand. Her sandals protected her from the harsh heat. She wondered if all the other women had similar thoughts as her, or if they were filled with the same kind of fear.

Lucia turned her head around and looked at the women behind her; a row of sad faces, most of them looking defeated. Lucia had been lucky in that she hadn't suffered the pain of being torn away from a husband or a family. Some of these women had been wives and mothers, but the Pharaoh didn't care. Everything was to serve him.

Some of the woman saw it as an honor, she knew. They held their heads high, looking forward to try to make themselves worthy of him. They saw it as a way to escape their life and fulfill their ambitions; being the Pharaohs' concubine with their freedom taken away, their only purpose in life to serve him in every way he wanted.

Lucia couldn't help but compare herself to others. She had always helped hunt and forage so she had a lithe figure. Although, in the last few years, she had matured; her hips had grown wider and her breasts had swelled. Her skin was naturally soft and her heart-shaped face was blessed with soft lips—the shape of palm leaves—and almond-shaped dark eyes. Her hair was long and black, reaching to the middle of her back, and her skin was tanned.

Some women had skin as dark as the night, while others were fair-skinned with blonde hair. It was amazing to see the variety of beauty on display. She couldn't imagine what exactly it was the Pharaoh was looking for, or why he hadn't found it yet.

Squinting in the sun, she looked ahead to see the rising city, its white buildings gleaming and making it difficult to look ahead. In the horizon, the pyramid rose; a testament to the Pharaoh's greatness and grandeur. It was a worthy place for a god to live.

They were led through the city. People came out to watch the procession, cheering them on and offering their blessings. In the outer tribes, the Pharaoh's reputation was one of ruthlessness and cruelty, one where he devastated lives without a second thought. Here, it was different. He took care of his subjects in the city. They all worshiped him as he demanded. In return, he made sure the crops were plentiful, and they were defended from any attacking enemies.

But, as Lucia passed them, she looked up and saw fear in their eyes. Parents held their daughters close, knowing that it was only through the whims of fate that the Pharaoh hadn't chosen them yet. If this search went on for years, it may well be that their daughters were chosen. For, it was inevitable that girls turned into women, and their existence took on an entirely different nature.

In their eyes, Lucia saw herself and how she had been young and innocent not too long ago. Now, her vision of the world had been corrupted; there was no going back to that sweet time when she was filled with naivety and an idea of the world that simply was not true.

A single tear rolled down her cheek, and she bowed her head to hide it from the guards. It was bad enough that she

was dragged along at their command, but quite another to
show them how much it affected her.

***

They shambled through the dusty streets of the city.
Occasionally, a good-hearted citizen brought some water
and fruit for them to eat. The guards quickly stepped in and
stopped them so not all the women got to enjoy some relief
for their dry lips and aching stomachs. Lucia only managed
to get a sip of water, but it brought her a world of relief.

"The Pharaoh will see to it that you are treated well before
you are presented to him," the guards said whenever
anyone from the crowd came up to offer the women a
blessing. Once they got the message, the people of the city
did not offer them anything else. None of them wanted to
earn the wrath of the Pharaoh.

As they moved through the city, the pyramid grew larger.
Its smooth sides were beautiful. She was left in awe of its
majesty. Surely, only a god could have had such a thing
built. Despite her feelings towards the Pharaoh, Lucia
appreciated the grandeur. It only increased when she was
led inside.

The air, shaded from the sun, was cooler in the pyramid. As
they moved into a large chamber, she found that the air was
scented with lavender. Carvings on the walls depicted
different battles and gods. Hieroglyphics were spread
around, offering testament to the greatness and strength of
the Pharaoh.

Some benches were spread around the chamber with jars of
water along with trays of grapes, bread, olives, and mugs of
wine. The woman eagerly nibbled at the food and drunk the

wine. They splashed water on their faces and bodies, washing themselves quickly, for none of them knew when they were going to be taken in to meet the Pharaoh.

Lucia's eyes darted around, as she split the white skin of a grape and felt the juice trickle down her throat. At first, she thought perhaps she might be able to make a friend, but nobody met her gaze. Each of them was scared. The ones who weren't fearful looked proud. Lucia tried to stand up straight, to act like them in the hope that perhaps she could project an air of confidence that could fool the Pharaoh. She immediately wilted, knowing that it was futile to even think of such a thing.

There was no way the Pharaoh would choose her. The guard that had placed his hand upon her was standing near the door, his gaze focused on her. She tried to ignore him, but she knew it was only a matter of time before she was in his arms, wrestling to get away. She hated the thought of being claimed by him. It was almost enough to make her vomit, but then a bell rang out. A man in a long white robe entered the chamber. He was a thin, gaunt man. When he spoke, his voice was as soft as the wind.

"You will now be presented to the Pharaoh. You are not to speak to him. You are not to touch him. If one of you is selected, you shall live in this kingdom with him. Those of you who are not selected will be free to return home," he said.

Every girl knew that he wasn't being completely honest. They were free to leave, but there was a price to be paid before they left. Suddenly, tension rose within Lucia's body. Her heart beat rapidly, as the chain of women were led through a narrow corridor to another chamber. In moments, she would be cast aside. That guard would lay his hands on her, and she'd never be able to escape.

She glanced at the surrounding area, hoping that she would find some way to escape, but there was no opportunity. They were taken through to a large hall that gleamed with gold. Goblets, plates and a gong hung by a high throne. Another table was filled with a feast. Lucia's stomach rumbled softly at the sight. She stood in line with the other woman as the Pharaoh approached. She almost gasped at the sight of him.

He was an impressive height, and his physique was that of a god. He wore a headdress draped over his head and shoulders. His thin beard was a line down the middle of his chin. His skin was tanned and muscular, so smooth that every inch of his masculine physique was on show. He wore gold bands around his wrists and a thin garment around his waist to protect his modesty. He held his head high. He had such a powerful aura about him, so much so that it commanded attention from everyone in the room. Lucia's breath was taken away by the sight of him. She was truly in the presence of a god.

He ignored the woman at first. Moving towards the table, he picked up a thick chunk of meat to chew on, then licked his fingers and murmured with delight. He turned to the women and folded his arms across his broad chest, studying them all intently.

A lump formed in her throat, for she knew this was the moment that would define her future. While she'd journeyed to this point, she had been determined to resist and had been convinced that she was never going to be chosen.

Now, something new sparked inside her; a wish to be chosen. That he was sent by the gods and imbued with divine energy seemed obvious to her now. There was something so alluring and enchanting about him, something that made her want to be with him and near him. Never had she felt so instinctively drawn to anyone else. She hadn't even known these feelings were possible. She wondered if all the other women were feeling the same thing.

The Pharaoh said not a word as he walked down the line, inspecting the women as he went along. His inscrutable gaze passed over each of them. He seemed to dismiss them as he went along. Lucia had no idea what he was looking for, but it was clear he wanted something specific.

When he came to her, Lucia resisted the temptation to look up, remembering what his attendant had said. Now that she was in the Pharaoh's presence, she didn't want to do anything to jeopardize her chances of being chosen by him. No matter how cruel and ruthless he was, she knew that her chances of happiness were much better with him than with his guards. A prickling sensation ran all over her body while she was in his presence. As she was under his gaze, she felt his power; it was intoxicating. She almost gasped as he stood a few inches away from her, such was the force of his presence. Her lips even trembled.

Then, in an instant, he passed her by and moved on to the next woman. Her heart sank. She knew she had missed her chance. She hadn't realized until that moment how devastated she would feel. She had only been in his presence for a mere moment and already she felt as though it was her destiny to serve him. She wasn't sure how she would be able to cope without being at his side.

She watched him move down the line, wishing that she had the courage to speak up and demand that he return to her. But what right did she have to demand things from a god?

Lucia closed her eyes, as she tried to prepare herself for the grim fate that awaited her. She hoped that, if she was limp enough and unenthusiastic, the guard would get bored with her quickly and toss her away so that she might crawl home and return to some semblance of normal life. Her thoughts were interrupted as the Pharaoh paused, turned, and returned to stand before her.

Lucia almost whimpered when he placed his hand under her chin and tilted her head up. She had no choice but to look at him. Her entire body trembled with fear, as she gazed up at his towering body. His eyes were the deepest green and, when she stared into them, she felt in thrall to him. His commanding nature was a natural part of him. She saw that now. It was his will that everyone bow to him, and his will was made real. She felt it in her heart and soul. He was her god. Her duty was to serve him.

She wondered if he saw that desire in her eyes because, immediately after this, he snapped his fingers and commanded them all to leave. All except her.

***

Lucia stood there as the guards released her from her shackles. The other women looked at her with envy. Lucia was confused. Had it really happened? Was she the one worthy of the Pharaoh?

The Pharaoh moved to his throne and studied her. Lucia wasn't sure what to do, but she knew not to do anything unless the Pharaoh wished it.

"Make me a plate of food and come here," he ordered.

Lucia bowed her head and hurried to the table where she picked up some meat, fruit, and bread to arrange neatly on the plate. She also poured him a mug of wine and brought it to him, offering it in supplication. He gestured to the wide arm of his throne. She placed her offerings on the arm. He ate some meat and slaked his thirst with wine. Red rivers ran down his chin before he wiped the trickling liquid away.

"Strip yourself of your garments," he said. Lucia nodded, swallowing a nervous lump in her throat. She quickly removed her clothes. As her virgin flesh was exposed, the Pharaoh leaned back in his throne and studied her.

"Turn around," he said. She did as he asked, allowing him to gaze upon every inch of her. Although she was still trembling, it was more with excitement than nervousness. She felt flattered that he was gazing on her naked flesh and hoped that she would please him.

She had never been in this position for anyone before, yet it seemed completely natural. With one look, one word, one gesture he had taken complete ownership of her body. She was willing to give it to him. It was as though something had snapped inside and filled her with the most glorious sense of well-being and contentment. When she finished a rotation, she gazed upon him again and hoped that she pleased him. He seemed to have a satisfied look upon his face.

"What is your name?" he asked.

"Lucia."

"Lucia. I have searched far and wide for a woman to fulfill my demands and satisfy my urges." He stood up and moved in front of her. Placing his hands upon her arms and turning her around, he examined her more closely. She felt entirely different to when the guard had put his hand upon her. His had been unwanted, but the Pharaoh's was where it belonged.

"Do you believe you can please me?"

"I will try my hardest, my Pharaoh. I…All I wish is to make you happy."

"This is good," he said, pursing his lips together. "Fall to your rightful place," he said, pointing to the floor.

Lucia sank to her knees without hesitation, hungry and eager to please him. He loomed above her like a giant. She knew him to be every inch a god. She reached out a hand, longing to place it upon his muscled thigh. She resisted at the last moment, afraid to touch him without his permission. He seemed to approve of this. He reached behind him and undid the strap that held the garment over his waist. Pulling it away, he revealed his erection. Lucia's mouth hung open.

"You truly are a god," she gasped, and her eyes flickered with exquisite delight, mixed with a little fear. "May I touch?" she asked.

"You may."

She reached out a hand and felt his strong, tight skin. Her slender fingers curled around his shaft and felt the rippling veins running around it. He was so thick and long that even with two hands she couldn't envelop his erection completely. Suddenly, she was struck with fear as she had never done anything like this before. She didn't want to disappoint him.

She was filled with natural urges; a sense that told her exactly what to do. She followed the path laid out for her by his moans and grunts. Each one brought with it a spark of delight within her mind. She loved the idea of pleasuring him, making herself worthy of him. She stroked him before he took her head in his hands and pulled her closer. Her open mouth was wide and her wet lips took him inside her. Heat filled her mouth and her tongue swirled, tasting his musky masculine organ until it dripped with her saliva.

She groaned as she closed her eyes, not knowing until that moment how complete she had felt until she had him in her mouth. She hadn't known how much she needed to serve a powerful man until she had gotten down on her knees in her rightful place. She touched him, caressed him, and found a rhythm where she took him deep in her throat. He seemed to surge with passion. Arousal swelled inside her, and she needed so badly to touch herself. One of her hands dropped to the middle of her thighs where she was hot and wet and sticky. A dazed delirium came over her. She moaned loudly but, almost as soon as she touched herself, she felt her hand being pulled away.

"No!" the Pharaoh yelled. "You do not touch yourself unless I give you permission."

He grabbed a fistful of hair and dragged her towards the throne. Lucia yelped. The pain was almost too much to bear, but then it began to blur with pleasure. Something inside her cracked.

He sat on the throne and pulled her head into his lap, burying her in his heat. He took his cock out and held it rigid as he smeared it over her face. She felt the wet heat slide across her lips and fought with him to try and catch it. She wanted to serve him with every fiber of her being. He bent her head down and forced his erection into her mouth. With both hands on her scalp, he took her head and drilled her downward, slamming her hard until her eyes rolled into the back of her head. Tears trickled down her cheeks.

Oh, it was a glorious feeling to be used by him, to be taken by a god. Through blurred vision, she looked up at the cruel, twisted snarl of his passion and knew that she could take anything he gave to her. His body was tight and tense. He wasn't giving her any respite as he locked her mouth around his erection and kept going. She felt him pulse and throb and release warm nectar that dripped down her throat. He pulled himself away.

"Before you swallow, open your mouth," he said. She did as he asked, feeling the heavy thick liquid settling on her tongue. She panted like a dog, as he dipped his finger in and scooped out some of the liquid. Then he smeared it across her cheek, marking his territory.

"Now turn around," he said. She did as he asked, placing her head and arms on the throne.

"You are mine now. I have claimed you to serve me and you shall do as I wish. You shall not be touched by any other man. You will always ask permission for anything that you do. Your only purpose in life now is to serve me, to worship me. Your life as you knew it is over. You are now reborn, you are now risen like the phoenix. I, your god, have resurrected you."

"Yes, my Pharaoh, I am yours, and I will do whatever you say. Use me as you wish. My body is yours to command.

Take out everything on me. There is nothing I will not do for you," she said.

The words seemed so natural, and her heart lifted as she spoke those words. They were a solemn vow, and she meant every single word. It was the most devout promise she had ever made, would ever make, but she knew her place was by her Pharaoh's side. There was nothing she wanted more in the world than to make him feel like the god that he was.

"I am glad to hear you are so willing to accept your new role. There are times when I will be angry," he said, and he walked over to throne where he picked up a flogger. He wrapped his hands around the handle. Lucia gulped, as she saw the strands clapping together. He walked behind her and brought it down across her back, leaving deep red marks. She cried out in pain, but again, it blurred with pleasure. There was nothing left but the ecstasy of anguish as a knot of pleasure uncoiled within her. He brought the flogger down with all his might, the instrument of passion made pain bloom as it burst upon her skin, and the lashes marked her body.

"There are times I will thirst," he threw the flogger down and reached over for the goblet of wine. He raised it above Lucia's head and tipped it upside down, letting the dark liquid flow onto her face and breasts. The wine dripped down her body and she gasped.

"There are times when I will be hungry," he said, and threw some meat on the floor. Lucia followed his pointed finger and picked up the meat, chewing it for him, showing him that she would do anything.

"There are times when I will want to watch," he said, this time he grabbed her hand and shoved it in between her legs. She yelped at the sensations. His grip was tight and left red marks on her wrist, but he used her hand to rub herself. She let the pleasure wash over her.

She closed her eyes and slipped a finger inside her, spreading her legs wide until she realized that he was no longer holding her. He had stepped back and was looking at her with pride, watching her pleasure herself, putting on a show for him. She exaggerated her movements and her moans. Warmth spread through her body, and soon enough, she felt the overwhelming, intoxicating feeling of pure bliss setting her heart aflame.

Before being with the Pharaoh, she never thought anything like this was possible. She felt her wetness and slipped so deep inside herself that she was reaching new places. The only thing more arousing would have been if Pharaoh had touched her as well. She whimpered and moaned and looked up at him with liquid eyes, begging him with her gaze to touch her.

"Taste yourself," he said.

Lucia obediently brought her hand to her mouth and placed her wet fingers between her lips. She sucked on them deeply, taking two into her mouth and feeling them with her tongue. She licked her fingers greedily, seeing how much it turned Pharaoh on. Already he was twitching and growing again, his impressive manhood rising once again to its full, rigid height.

"Get on the table," he said, promptly swiping his arm to push everything off it. The plates and wine clattered to the floor. It seemed that nothing was going to get in the way of the Pharaoh and what he wanted. Lucia climbed onto the table and lay there, looking at the glyphs and pictures around her, all of them paying tribute to the Pharaoh who was god.

"There is one other thing I must do before I claim you properly. Everywhere you go people must see that you belong to me. You must bear my mark, always. I take you now until your death. You will serve me for life, and I must brand you so that everyone knows you are my property."

Lucia gulped, the thought of being branded was a scary one. Yet, it also filled her with an overwhelming sense of excitement. The god wanted to mark her, wanted to make her his. She knew it would last a long time. She would never have to want for anything ever again. She would never have to feel scared or alone. She would go wherever the Pharaoh wanted her, and she would always have his presence in her life. Even when they were apart, she could look down at his mark and draw strength from the image of his ownership. She nodded.

"I am ready to receive your mark," she groaned.

The heights of pleasure were playing havoc with her mind. She could barely think straight, but she wanted this more than anything else in the world. She rolled her bottom lip under her tongue as he stepped aside, his body exposed and naked. He had no shame at all, nor should he; for, he was as perfect as any man who walked the earth. She watched him as he went beside his throne and pulled up a pole from a pot. She heard some bubbling and the end of the pole gleamed gold, and the metal made the air sizzle. As he returned, she could feel the heat of it as he let it hover over her skin.

"With this brand you are completely mine," he said, and pressed the burning metal into her skin. Her flesh hissed as the heat seared his mark into her. She gasped and writhed in pain. A whimper flew from her mouth, as blinding heat washed through her. The mark ran deeper than just her flesh, as though he had marked her soul.

The brand glowed orange and tears trickled from her cheeks. The pain was overwhelming. She shook and trembled as she looked down at her heart and saw the flesh sizzle. The mark of his symbol was golden. She was forever his. Looking at it made her feel important and flattered. She was groggy as she looked up to him, devoted and obedient. He found the whole act arousing.

"I am yours, completely and utterly, Pharaoh. You own me. You control me. You can do whatever you like to me," she said, trying her best to ignore the pain that throbbed in her burned flesh.

The Pharaoh's eyes gleamed with hunger, as he put his hand around her throat and looked down at her mark. He climbed on top of the table, his muscular physique easily able to control her. She couldn't have resisted even if she wanted to, but there was no way she wanted to resist. He pushed her legs aside.

She watched him tower over her. He groped her body as though she was just a toy, leaving deep imprints where his fingers met her flesh. She writhed and gasped underneath him, making the effort to appear as though she wanted to get away. She had seen how he liked it when she fought, and when he had to overpower her.

His grip tightened on her throat until it was harder to breathe. Pharaoh licked his lips and gazed down at her most intimate area, using his other hand to tease her. First, he dragged his fingers up her inner thigh, and then grazed the fine hairs before he pressed his palm against her. A new world of delight was revealed to her.

Her eyes clamped shut and she inhaled as much as she could, although she was still struggling to breathe. Then, he slipped his finger inside her and curled it back and forth. It was long and slender and reached into the deepest part of her. She groaned as she became overwhelmed with the sensations crashing through her body. Her skin prickled with sweat and a tingling sensation rippled outwards, beginning from the pit of her groin where the heat burned most fiercely. At first, Pharaoh was gentle, but that soon changed.

Lucia had no idea that it would have been like this. She had touched herself before but she had never been touched by anyone else. Although her touch had been pleasurable, this was something else. Someone else being in control of her body and her not knowing what was going to happen next elicited a great feeling of excitement.

Her heart raced and a smile broke over her face as Pharaoh rammed his fingers inside her, driving them into her and making her entire body shake as though she was just a mere puppet. Her legs instinctively shut as the orgasm crashed over her, making her entire body try to curl up into a ball, but Pharaoh wasn't done with her yet.

He used his powerful muscles to pry her legs open and stare at the wetness awaiting him. She watched as his huge erection came closer and closer, the heat sliding against her slick thighs. She was filled with fear as she wondered how she was ever going to take him inside her. He pressed down on her throat as he thrust into her, and her mind cracked. She went limp as he started to fuck her.

Her hands splayed over the side of the table and long, low, guttural moans escaped her throat. Pharaoh loomed over her, every muscle tense as his face snarled and twisted with ecstatic delight. Lucia forced herself to keep her eyes open so that she could gaze into the eyes of a god as he made love to her.

No, not love. This was something more than love. This was dominance.

She was his. No sweeter thought brought her more cascading pleasure. Pharaoh pounded her body so hard, she thought the table was going to crack underneath them. Breath was squeezed from her throat. Yet, another orgasm ran through her from head to toe before the Pharaoh used all his powerful strength for the fury of his own release; using her to make him feel good.

He thrust powerfully with every inch of his body, seeming ready to tear her apart inside. She reached up, daring to touch his body. She was in heaven. He came with the force of a god. A powerful roar echoed through the chambers of the pyramid and sweat dripped from his body, sizzling on her skin.

With a violent jerk, he released himself. The warmth spread through her, dripping down her thighs afterwards. Her throat was bruised, and she was covered in his marks, but she had never looked so beautiful.

She gasped for breath as she sat up; a writhing, wrecked mess. Pharaoh admired his handiwork while wearing a smirk on his face.

"Clean yourself. I shall have use for you later," he said and then returned to his throne after placing a hand upon her cheek and bestowing a kiss upon her.

Lucia bowed her head and cleaned herself with water. She did not put on her clothes, preferring to stay naked so that Pharaoh could enjoy the sight of her body. She sank to his feet and remained in her rightful place, waiting for the moment when he was ready to use her again.

Valentine's Day was approaching and, so far, the year had been gloomy. February was usually a grey month, but this year it had seemed especially so. The year had started so brightly for Victoria, with both she and her husband, Dan, vowing to pull themselves out of the rut that they had fallen into.

She supposed it was something that every married couple endured at one time or another. Sometimes the whole idea of monogamy seemed flawed because humans needed variety and, at a certain point, being with the same person day in, day out became tiresome. There were no surprises any longer, and it had been at Christmas when they had realized they were in trouble. Months had passed without them making love and, in truth, neither of them had actually realized it until it had suddenly occurred to Victoria. The ache in her body wasn't as powerful as it had once been, but it was still there, and she had always believed that it was the job of a romantic partner to help inspire that spark. Unfortunately, Dan didn't seem to be all that interested, either.

In the past, whenever circumstances had dictated a break in sex, they had always come back together and had a furious, passionate session where they expressed their lust and love for each other. On this occasion, though, it was a silent, dull affair where it seemed as though they were simply taking care of the biological needs of their bodies rather than anything more spiritually transcendent. Somewhere along the way, their relationship had lost the edge that made it exciting.

It made for a lot of soul searching over that Christmas.

Victoria and Dan were only in their early forties, so it wasn't as though they were over the hill, and she didn't believe they should be heading to a sedentary life just yet. And yet, it felt as though they were on an inexorable journey to nothingness. The worst thing was that Dan just didn't seem to care.

"I'm sorry, but I can't just conjure up these feelings inside me as though I'm a magician. It's not you, and it's not me; it's just one of those things that ends up happening in life. I still love you. I still want to make you happy, and you still make me happy. It doesn't take away what we have together, either. We've built a life together, and I'm proud of everything we've accomplished.

"Does sex really have to be such a big deal? Does it have to define us like this?" he had asked during one fight they'd had after Christmas.

It had started off as a discussion, but frustration and resentment had set in, and it had quickly become a full-blown argument.

"Yes, it does. Because, without sex, we're more than friends. And it's a natural part of life.

"Don't you get tired of not feeling as good as we used to? Do you remember there was a time when you couldn't keep your hands off me? And I know it's unrealistic to suggest that we're like that all the time, but I don't think it's unreasonable to ask that we can at least have glimpses of that part of our lives, do you?"

"No, I suppose not, but then it comes back to the point where I say that I don't know how to make myself feel something that's not there. I don't want to have to feel like I'm forcing it. I want it to happen naturally and organically."

"You say that, but then it never happens naturally or organically!" Victoria cried.

Dan didn't have much to say to that.

"Do you even find me attractive anymore?" Victoria asked.

"Don't say that. Of course I do," Dan said immediately, reaching out to put an arm around her waist. Victoria, however, backed away, feeling vulnerable.

She looked at Dan, remembering the way the two had been when they had first met as fresh-faced twenty-year-olds, with the whole world ahead of them and so many hopes and dreams. Together, they had thought they could conquer the world. Instead, like so many others before them, they had capitulated under the weight of bills, a mortgage, and the endless monotony of jobs that didn't inspire any passion. Perhaps that was just the thing of it all—they were tired of life; mentally and physically drained from churning through the wheels of society.

Back at the beginning, Victoria had been slender, with curves in all the right places, and thick, long brown hair. Her eyes had sparkled, and her skin had been supple. Over the years, however, as she had lost her interest in running, she had put on some weight and her hair had thinned. She had also chopped it shorter, because it had been too heavy for her to carry, so now it came to the base of her neck, resting on her shoulders.

Dan had been muscular and lithe, with a swimmer's physique, but he, too, had let himself go. The middle-aged comfort had created a paunch, and his once thick hair had thinned to wispy strands. They were ordinary mortals, and there was no magical elixir to give them more vigor.

"It doesn't feel like it, is all I'm saying. I just wish that I was enough to get you in the mood. I know sometimes you're tired or you don't feel like it, but that doesn't mean there's no chance of anything happening. I just miss being close to you," she admitted.

Then she fell into his lap, and they made love again. It was sweet and tender, but afterward, Victoria ended up staying awake, staring at the ceiling while Dan slept happily.

A quick roll was enough for him, it seemed, but she wanted more, and it wasn't even more out of sex. She wanted more out of life.

The more she thought about it, the more she realized that there had been something profound missing from their relationship for a long time, and it had taken her a while to think about it.

Dan seemed to accept there was a problem, but he didn't want to make the effort to figure things out. He just seemed to think that acknowledging the problem was enough to solve it, but that was never going to be the case.

Over Christmas, there had been plenty of discussions, and it had gotten to the point where Victoria seemed to always be the one that was raising her concerns. They had stayed up late at night and had gone over the same things again and again.

"This is starting to get annoying," Dan said.

"Oh, I'm sorry if my feelings are annoying to you,"
Victoria replied.

"I didn't mean it like that. We just seem to be going over
the same things repeatedly and nothing ever changes."

"That's the problem! Nothing does change! I thought that
Christmas might be different because there's always magic
in the air, but even that passed by without any progress. I
need things to change, Dan. I just … I can't go on like this.
It's stressing me out, and it's getting to the point where I'm
feeling anxious about sex, and I really don't want to reach
the stage where we don't even talk about it."

"But talking about it all the time adds stress to it.
Sometimes, it's better to go with the flow and let things get
figured out by themselves, but you keep drilling these
things into my head, and I can't think of sex without feeling
stressed now."

"Oh, great, so now it's my fault? What I am supposed to
do, just shut up and bear it? Just get used to the status
quo?" The tone of her voice was strong, and her words
were heavy.

She glared at Dan, her eyes wide, her face flushed with
fury, and her hair wild. She expected him to fight back, but
he didn't.

He slumped his shoulders and dropped his head, sighing
heavily and shaking his head. "I'm sorry that I'm not the
man you want me to be."

"That's it," Victoria said, snapping her fingers. A moment
of realization hit her as she figured out what had been
missing.

"What's it?" Dan asked glumly. "Have you figured out that we're at the end of the line? I don't want things to end, Victoria. Maybe we can figure something out. If you need to have sex with someone else … I don't know … maybe we can find someone. It has been unfair of me to deny you what you need. You have these desires, and if I can't fulfill them, then you should find someone who can."

"Don't be stupid," Victoria said. "I don't want anyone else, and I don't want to invite anyone else into our marriage. I don't want to leave you, either. I love our life; I just want it to be the best it can be. I want us to know what it's like to be happy again.

"I know what's missing, and I hope you don't take this the wrong way, Dan, but you used to take control. You remember, when we were younger and you would sometimes just grab me and fuck me whenever you wanted? You were just so … masculine, and you've lost something of that over the years. Maybe a life of domesticity has taken away that edge. If we could rediscover that, maybe things would be different. Maybe what you need is to feel empowered again."

Dan was uncertain, but he did end up admitting that he had been feeling less able to influence the universe, and it might have bled into his personal life.

On New Year's Eve, they had decided to make a resolution to rekindle their passion.

Victoria felt better at knowing exactly what the problem was, because now she could work on a solution. Dan felt better, too, and the year seemed like it was going to be a good one.

However, aside from a few, brief lovemaking sessions at the beginning of the year, it seemed difficult for them to break the habit of being isolated and separate. Dan tried to get into a masculine, powerful mood, but he never quite seemed to be able to push through the barriers and give in to his beastly instincts. Victoria tried acting submissively and coy and innocent, but it never worked properly. Dan always held back, pulling away from her, and she didn't know what to do.

She didn't want to give up on her marriage, nor did she want to live an unfulfilled life. She loved Dan, but even love had its limits, and she was reaching hers.

*

"I just don't know what to do," she said to her friend Lizzie as she confessed her problems. "I don't want to leave him, but I can't go on like this for much longer. He actually did suggest that I should find another man to give me what I need, but I just find the idea of that so wrong."

"Would it be the worst thing in the world, though?" Lizzie asked. "People need different things. Sometimes, I think the worst thing in the world is this lie that people have to stay with one person for the rest of their lives. Think about how many divorces would be avoided if people were allowed to indulge their desires once in a while?"

"I'm not sure about that. I don't like the idea of having sex with someone I don't have any emotional attachment to, or worse, developing an emotional attachment to someone who isn't my husband."

Lizzie shrugged. "Jane did it."

Jane was someone else who worked with Victoria. Although Victoria had been so consumed with her own problems that she hadn't been privy to this particular morsel of gossip.

"Really?" Victoria gasped.

"Oh yes, but it wasn't on the up and up. She said that things were so bad with her and Bob that she ended up finding some guy online. At first, it was just chatting over text. She called it interactive porn."

"Didn't she feel guilty at all?" Victoria wondered.

"I think she did at first, but then it just became too easy and felt too good. Bob was unaware, and she didn't seem to think he'd even care if he did find out. So, she kept going and said that, even through texting, this guy turned her on more than Bob had over the past five years.

"Maybe you could try something similar? It's not really the same thing if you're just talking to people, is it?"

"I don't know. It feels like a line could be blurred, and I'd be afraid of things getting out of hand. Is she still doing this?"

"Actually, she ended up meeting the guy in person, and then she decided to tell Bob, because she couldn't help herself from wanting to be with this other man. He didn't share her opinion that texting was just a bit of fun, and they had a lot of arguments. Now I don't think they're living together at the moment …" Lizzie trailed off.

Victoria cupped her mug of coffee and hunched her body forward. "That's exactly what I don't want to happen. It all just seems like a slippery slope, and even if I was going to find another man, I don't know if I would be able to go through with it. I'd just feel too guilty."

"Even if you had Dan's blessing?"

Victoria nodded. "He just doesn't seem to understand that it's not just these physical needs I want to feel again; it's the emotional ones, as well. I want to feel close to him, not to anyone else."

"I suppose the other thing you could do is go to marriage counseling or even a sex therapist," Lizzie suggested.

Victoria grimaced.

"I know there's a certain stigma to it, but if they can help, surely it's worth a go?"

"Maybe," Victoria sighed out. "I'm just so frustrated that this has been going on for so long now, and it doesn't feel like it's ever going to get resolved. We can talk and talk about it as often as I want, but it's not going to change anything. Things get better for a little while, and then they just fall back into the same pattern again. I don't want to be locked into this back and forth for the next few years. It's exhausting. It should be simple, you know? When did sex become so complicated? It should be the most natural thing in the world."

"It is when two people are in harmony, but that's your problem, I guess. Or, more accurately, it's Dan's problem. I don't really have any extra advice for you, except that maybe, if this is exhausting you, then you should take a step back and stop bringing it up. You've said all you can say, so now the ball is in Dan's court."

Victoria sighed yet again then took a sip of her coffee, feeling the warm liquid slide down her throat, leaving a pleasing, satisfying sensation in the depth of her body. "It's all well and good saying that, but I'm worried that, if I don't say anything, nothing is ever going to get resolved. We're just going to end up avoiding the problem completely, so it's on me to keep fighting for what I want."

But she knew she could only fight for so long.

*

After her conversation with Lizzie, Victoria thought about indulging her desires with another man. She didn't want to, and she didn't particularly feel comfortable doing it, but she needed something to help uncoil the tension in her body. She tried to tell herself that, if Dan said it was okay, then she was allowed to do it and didn't have to feel guilty about it.

She wasn't willing to go as far as Jane and actually talk with another man, even online. That veered too far toward adultery for her liking, but she happily watched porn and studied the masculine form, imagining what it would be like to be fucked by another man.

She found a category of wife-sharing videos, where the husbands watched while the wives were being pounded by another man, a stranger. It seemed antithetical to her that someone should be turned on by watching their partner with another person, but these men certainly enjoyed it.

While she was aware that it was porn, so it was difficult to tell what was real and what wasn't, she did some research afterward and found out that it was a particular fetish for some people, and that the men often shared their wives as a show of power, for it was the ultimate display of confidence to give her to someone and know that she was going to return no matter what.

Still, Victoria didn't like the idea of being passed around like a piece of meat. She wanted Dan to be strong, but not to be abusive and degrading. So, in the end, she didn't think sharing herself with another man was for her … Although, if it got Dan turned on, then she might be willing to try it just to kick-start his sexual desire.

There was definitely something not right, and although, in her insecure moments, she worried that it was something to do with her, she had to believe him when he reassured her that it wasn't, that it was just something about the way he viewed the world.

She was sure that there was some secret combination that she could find that would unlock his desire, but it was just a matter of finding that combination. She thought about sharing porn with him … and even indulged in the idea of welcoming another woman. Perhaps it was a case where he needed some variety—a new body in front of him. If she was there, it wouldn't be cheating. Still, the thought of him with another woman filled her with the same unsettling feeling as the thought of being with another man did.

She hated to admit it, but she was thoroughly powerless in the situation, and that was perhaps the worst thing of all.

This all happened in the month of January. By the time February rolled around, she had given up talking to Dan about it. Every time she brought it up, it descended into an argument, and she was tired of fighting about it, especially because nothing ever got resolved. The brief flush of arousal that occurred after one of their "discussions" wasn't worth all the stress and hassle that occurred during the build-up, so Victoria simply stopped caring. After all, what was the point when Dan didn't care either?

Night after night passed. At first, Victoria hoped that Dan might realize she had lost interest and would start to fight back, trying to reclaim what had been lost. Maybe, she thought, once he realized that she wasn't going to fight for them anymore, he would start fighting. It turned out to be a forlorn hope, as she had expected. Dan didn't mention anything about sex or even make any kind of move.

Part of her wondered if there was something medically wrong with his body, but during one of her sleepless nights, she noticed that he had an erection, so his body was still capable of having these reactions; it was just the case that his mind wasn't.

Even just seeing his body in that state was enough to arouse her, which spoke to how deprived she was.

Victoria rolled her bottom lip under her teeth and reached out, wanting to feel the heat and the hardness. But, when her fingers brushed the outline, he turned around, and she was left dismayed. Even in sleep, he wasn't interested, and she was left feeling utterly desolate and isolated.

The days were long, but the nights were longer. She ached for something more, yet she wasn't getting it.

This distance between them started to affect their day-to-day lives, as well. Even when they weren't doing anything sexual, she felt unfulfilled, for it felt as though there was a wedge between them. If she lost that emotional closeness, as well as the physical closeness, she didn't know what she was going to do. She started to feel empty, less than herself, and now that she had stopped herself from talking about the situation, she wasn't sure what she was going to be able to do to affect the future.

She had stunned herself into silence, and now she was unable to bring forth the words she needed. It was as though she wanted to scream but had no mouth.

The horror dawned on her that this might be what the rest of her life would be like. She didn't know if she could carry on another year like this, or another decade. The future seemed to stretch out ahead of her in one endless stream of monotony, without excitement and passion. It was cruel to be shackled to such a fate. The worst thing above all else was that she felt as though it was a fate she had to face alone.

When she and Dan had gotten married, they had vowed to move through life together and face every challenge together. That was the whole point of marriage, after all—it was a partnership where you had to support each other and be there for each other. Somewhere along the way, however, they had become two people living together rather than a married couple. And, as the shadows of sorrow surrounded her, Victoria came to the realization that she had to leave.

The gloomy weather outside reflected the sorry state of her heart. It was just a matter of time before she was going to tell Dan the bad news. It seemed awful to know that the life she had built was going to crumble into ash, yet she didn't feel as though she had any choice. It had gotten to the point now where she couldn't see them reclaiming what they had once had.

She had thought it was dormant inside them and all they needed to do was look deep enough inside themselves to find what they were missing. Sadly, it was clear to her that what she was looking for just didn't exist anymore. Somewhere along the way, it had faded away into dust and had blown into the wind.

Ultimately, she decided that she was going to tell Dan on Valentine's Day. It seemed darkly suitable to wait until then and gave her a deadline to work up the courage. She was afraid that, if she didn't set herself such a deadline, she was going to end up letting the feelings linger until nothing happened.

The problem was that she didn't know how to bring up the sad news. Strings of words twisted and twirled through her mind. The end of a marriage was an enormous thing, and there were moments when she doubted herself.

Was she being unreasonable? Was she wrong in wanting to end her marriage because of, when it came down to it, a lack of sex? Maybe she should have tried to accept the inevitable like Dan had. At least then she wouldn't have to face the grim abyss of the world alone.

No, she had to be strong. She wanted a relationship where she felt as though her problems mattered and were taken seriously by her partner. Dan hadn't been able to do that for a long time.

He didn't even speak about Valentine's Day. Usually, they planned some sort of special evening. So, once again, Victoria decided to not mention it unless he did. She wanted to see if he would plan anything of his own accord or even acknowledge that something was happening. She was hoping for a surprise dinner reservation, or perhaps even a new dress waiting for her when she awoke. As the days passed by, though, it became clear that he wasn't going to do anything.

However, on Valentine's Day, she awoke to an empty bed. Dan had already left for work. Victoria wondered if this was a foreshadowing of the rest of her life.

She stretched out her limbs and made full use of the bed, but she would much rather have been curled up with Dan, sharing the warmth of his body.

The whole day was filled with anguish as she worried about what was going to happen when she got home. She hoped against hope that Dan would send her some flowers at work, or even just a greeting card—something to show that he remembered and cared.

To see other women in the office get sent flowers stabbed her in the heart, and as the day wore on, she became resigned to the fact that she was going to have to begin a new life alone.

She left the office depressed and made the long journey home, to a place that was filled with resentment and emptiness.

***

When Victoria returned home, she saw that the lights were on and paused before going in, dreading the thought of seeing Dan, because she knew, once she stepped over the threshold, there would be no going back. Their marriage would be over. She couldn't put it off forever, though, so she opened the door and heard the sound of Dan moving inside.

She went into the lounge, where a glass of wine was waiting for her, as well as a big wrapped box on the coffee table. Hope sprang inside her, although she was almost too afraid to hope. There was a sense that this was too little, too late.

Dan emerged and smiled at her. He kissed her on the cheek then guided her to the couch, handing her the glass of wine.

As she took a sip, the intoxicating bubbles rose through her body and made her feel all tingly inside. It took the edge off her day, and she relaxed into the couch, willing to see where this was going.

"I know that I haven't been too attentive recently, and I also know that we made a New Year's resolution, and that we haven't been the best at sticking to it. It's something that I take responsibility for, and I'm sorry that I haven't been as present as I could be.

"I want you to know that things have been on my mind. I know we haven't talked about things for a while, and partly that's because we never seem to accomplish anything when we do speak about it. I had to look deep into myself to realize what was going on.

"Something you said struck a chord with me, about how I wasn't the man I used to be. I took a long, hard look at myself and realized you were right. I have lost myself over the years. I do remember a time when we couldn't keep our hands off each other. Believe me; I wanted to recapture that feeling, but I didn't understand what was happening inside me, or why I couldn't summon the feelings that used to be so powerful. I think, honestly, I have been made so weary with life."

His words had shocked her. She certainly hadn't expected to come home to an appreciative husband who was willing to reflect on his thoughts and tell her that he had been working on fixing things. Still, it wasn't enough to mend the wounds that had appeared.

"I appreciate you saying that, Dan," Victoria said. "But I'm not sure it's the right time. I needed you to tell me this months ago. Why has it taken you so long?"

"I'm sorry, Victoria. Like I said, I've been doing a lot of soul searching, but I think I know what we can do to make things better."

"Dan … I think it's just too late. The chance has gone. We've spent so long talking about things that now doing something about it doesn't feel right. It's just going to end up leading us down the same path, and I'm tired of making the same mistakes. I'm tired of going through this cycle of despair. I want it to end."

"And it will end; I promise you that. After tonight, nothing is going to be the same again."

He was so earnest in his belief that Victoria really wanted to share that feeling, but she had been burned too many times.

Perhaps it was a symptom of her perseverance, or it was a deeper part of her love that had survived the onslaught of emotions. However, she was willing to give him yet another chance, although she promised herself that this would be the last one.

"What's happening tonight, then?" she asked.

Dan proudly smiled and picked up the box, handing it to her. It was heavier than she had expected. She had no idea what was inside, as the box was blank, the outside giving no clue as to the contents.

"Open it," he said.

She doubted there was some miracle cure that was going to save her marriage, but she opened the gift, nonetheless, and ripped away the paper, leaving it in shreds on the floor. Then Victoria's eyes were agape with the sight of new toys.

"What is this?" she gasped.

"It's a bondage set. I was thinking about the nature of power and how our sex life has been lacking something. I thought maybe we could try some of these toys. It might help awaken something in me," he said. "I'm sorry if it's too weird."

Victoria ran her eyes around the box of toys. She saw handcuffs, a whip, thick, black rope, a blindfold, a gag, and many other things that she couldn't even begin to describe. Just looking at it made her insides churn, and she felt an old stirring of passion. It was as though something had been awakened inside her. She thought there might just be a chance for her marriage after all.

She plucked out the blindfold from the box and held it over her face. Then she turned to Dan. "Does this work for you?"

"You have no idea," he replied. His words were tinged with an intensity that hadn't been present for a long time.

Suddenly, he was upon her, dragging her by the wrist upstairs. It was as though a switch had been flicked and a spark burst into life inside him.

She carried the magical box of toys with her.

They still had a lot of time to make up for but, in that first moment, it seemed as though she had her husband back.

*

When they were in the bedroom, Victoria emptied all the toys onto the bed. As they tumbled out, she stretched out her hands to grab a few of them. Meanwhile, Dan ran his hand over her back and stroked her hair.

"Which ones of these would you like to use first?" she asked.

Dan examined them. Then he picked out the gag, a collar and leash, and the handcuffs. But first, she had to get naked.

She peeled off her clothes and, as she did so, she reached out and felt Dan's body, stroking him, caressing him, before she dropped her hands between his legs and she felt how hard he was. It was a glorious return, and one that she had been longing to witness for so damned long.

Once she was naked, Dan let his hands roam all around her before pulling her hands above her head and handcuffing her to one of the bars of the headboard.

Victoria struggled, and as soon as she realized she couldn't move, a wave of pure ecstasy swept through her. Her mouth opened in a silent moan, but she was quickly silenced as Dan tied the gag around her mouth. It bit into her lips, and she moaned again.

"Just cry out loudly and shake your head if you want me to stop," he said.

Part of her wondered where he had suddenly learned all these things, but she wasn't going to question it. All she wanted was to enjoy this new, electric pleasure that crackled through her body and made her feel lighter than air.

Dan then clasped the collar around her neck. It made her feel utterly owned and submissive. It was this sinking feeling that she embraced wholly. Her blood turned to syrup, and she felt as though she was going to melt into a puddle of lust.

Dan growled, his hands hard, digging into her skin. She watched him carefully as he rooted through the toys and picked up a flogger. Its handle was thick and the strands looked so harmless.

He dragged it down her body. The fingers of the flogger felt so nice against her skin. They made her shiver when they traversed the curves of her ample breasts and stimulated her nipples. Then she shuddered as Dan took it down across her burning inner thighs.

He noticed how she writhed and seemed to take a great deal of delight in knowing that he had power over her body, that with one flick of his wrist, he could make her writhe and moan and cause pleasure to crash through her body.

Just as she was getting used to the comfortable feeling of the flogger against her skin and the warm feeling lingering over her flesh, Dan brought the flogger back with a flick of his wrist then brought it crashing down over her thigh. The blinding pain flashed in her mind but blurred with pleasure, creating an entirely new, intoxicating cocktail. She knew she would never be able to get enough of it.

Dan brought the flogger crashing down over and over again. Pain stung her breasts and stomach, her neck, her arms. It was all over her body, and she was consumed by this sensation.

Her eyes glistened with sweet tears, and she looked through her blurred vision to see Dan lashing out at her. His body was rigid with tension, every part of him, and she felt desire sweep through her. He was the epitome of manliness.

He had reclaimed his primal destiny, his entire body bristling with masculine power and strength.

Her heart thundered in her chest as he pulled her legs apart and started to play with her so confidently, like he hadn't played with her in years. Fingers danced wildly inside her. The handcuffs clanked against the bed. She struggled and writhed. Her muffled moans couldn't break through the gag. This submission sent her to the moon and back.

Dan threw the flogger away and loomed over her, so tall and powerful. She could see nothing apart from him. He was her everything.

His chest heaved. His body was slick with sweat. His face was twisted into a snarl as he unleashed all his strength. He groped her body then held her waist as he plunged inside her with the full force of his body, but he wasn't done yet. He grabbed the leash and curled it around her first then pulled.

Victoria was completely at his mercy as she felt him take control of her. She felt his desire, his strength. Her body arched under his weight and his passion, her soul buckling with the sheer power of his lust. Pain was etched upon her face, and it seemed that this was the edge that had been missing.

Dan pulled so tightly on the collar that it almost choked her, which seemed to be what he needed to get over the brink of orgasm. It was what she needed, as well. To feel him so hard and ardent inside her, to feel how much he wanted her was enough to send her into ecstatic delirium. She felt such an intense supernova heat burning inside her that it almost made for all the dormant years.

Almost.

They still had a lot of catching up to do, but their marriage had been saved.

It was Rachel's 18th birthday. Her parents had thrown her a party at their house. It was night and the stars were twinkling brightly in the sky. The pale moon shone down upon them, and there was a jovial atmosphere in the house. Each room was filled with friends and family, and everyone was having a good time.

Rachel was a petite young woman with a heart-shaped face, tawny brown hair that came down to her shoulders, a slender figure with curves around her breasts and hips. She stood at 5'4", so she was used to looking up at everyone around her. She had sparkling blue eyes that were tinged with flecks of green, and everyone always told her that she looked younger than her age. She wasn't sure if that was a compliment or not, although everyone assured her that one day she would be glad for it.

She wore a red dress with straps that hung on her shoulder. The dress clung to her, and was without a doubt the sexiest, most grown up thing she had ever worn. Rachel certainly felt like an adult wearing it, and she'd noticed ardent stares from the men and boys present. Rachel felt her cheeks burning because she wasn't used to this sort of attention. In recent months, as she'd grown, she'd found that friends who had been entirely platonic now seemed to have a different energy about them; they looked at her with hunger in her eyes. Everything was changing and she wasn't quite sure how to cope with it. It felt as though she was on a rollercoaster and there was no way to hit the brakes.

But she took a deep breath and told herself to enjoy the party. She'd only ever get one 18th birthday, and she was determined not to let it go to waste. This was the beginning of the rest of her life, and she wanted to make a good start.

She was with her group of friends idly talking about their plans for the summer when she noticed her father open the door and hug the man who stood there. Rachel's heart skipped a beat, and her skin tingled. It felt as though the temperature in the room had just shot up a few degrees, and sweat prickled on her flesh. The man who walked into their home was Daniel, an old family friend. He was tall, standing just over six feet. He had jet black hair which he always kept neatly cut, twinkling eyes, and a trim figure. He played racquetball and was an avid runner. He had a kind smile, deep brown eyes, and very big hands. Rachel thought herself odd for noticing that about him, but it made her feel queasy inside.

For a few years now, Rachel had harbored a crush on this man even though he was her father's friend. She knew it was inappropriate, but she couldn't help herself. There was just something about him that sparked desire from within, not that she had ever shared this secret with anyone. He was 40, old enough to be her father, and she doubted that he'd be interested in her anyway. She'd looked with envy at the women she'd seen him with over the years, and she was glad that he had come to her party alone. None of them had seemed good enough for him.

She almost wished that she could rip out her desire for him because it wasn't healthy. She couldn't imagine what her parents would say if they found out. They could never find out. Daniel and her father exchanged a few words and then Daniel scanned the room. His gaze found Rachel, and for a moment their eyes locked. Rachel gasped, breath catching in her throat, and her eyes darted away. Daniel seemed amused by this.

He came over to her, and Rachel's friends drifted away, although they all gave him looks of desire. It wasn't just her who found him attractive, but Rachel knew that only she truly wanted him.

She blinked and inhaled deeply, trying to compose herself. She told herself that it wasn't a natural desire and that she had to stop thinking of him in these terms, but when he was standing in front of her, towering above her, his musky aftershave playing havoc with her senses, she felt as though she was going to melt.

"Rachel, happy birthday, you look beautiful," he said, leaning in to give her a kiss on the cheek. His lips brushed her flesh and his hand wrapped around the small of her back briefly. Her body yielded to his touch and arched, and then he pulled away. The contact had been all too brief, but those few moments in his arms had been heavenly.

She smiled and thanked him. There was so much she wanted to say, but the words were getting all jumbled and it felt as though her mouth was filled with marbles.

"Are you having a good time?" he asked

"Oh, yes, it's wonderful to have all my friends and family here."

"That's good. I got you a little something," he said, and reached into his pocket, pulling out a small wrapped gift. Rachel's eyes widened as she accepted the gift. Their hands brushed as she took it, and desire inflamed inside her. She tore away the wrapping and opened the velvet box inside.

"Oh, Daniel, it's beautiful," she said. Inside the box was a sparkling golden pendant, a heart that was lined with twinkling jewels. It was the most beautiful thing she had ever seen, and she was sure that it must have cost him a fortune. "You shouldn't have!"

"Of course I should have. You're only 18 once, and you deserve something special. A beautiful woman needs beautiful jewelry, may I?"

She nodded and turned her back to him. He took the pendant from the box and moved her hair away. She could feel the concentration, and his hot breath danced over her exposed neck. It was an innocent act, yet Rachel felt completely vulnerable to him and heat spread throughout her body. Nobody else would think anything untoward about it, but she couldn't help feeling as though she and this handsome older man were doing something incredibly intimate.

He clasped the necklace around her neck without any trouble at all and then he placed his hands on her shoulders and turned her around. Rachel's hair fell back over her neck and she was standing before him, looking at him looking at her. For a moment, she was convinced she saw something like desire in his eyes, but she told herself that she must have been dreaming.

"It looks perfect," he said, taking the pendant in between his fingers. His hand rested against her chest, and she wondered if Daniel could feel the powerful beating of her heart or if he found the rise of her breasts alluring. The air seemed to sizzle between them, and in that moment, it felt as though anything could happen, but then he stepped away and said that he was going to talk with her father and the tension diminished. For the rest of the night, Rachel thought about that moment and wondered if, in some other universe, the world would have melted away leaving the two of them alone together.

***

Rachel was barely able to concentrate for the rest of the party. She spent time with her friends, but her gaze was always darting about the room, fixated on Daniel. When she didn't seem him, she panicked, worried that he had gone without saying goodbye, and when she saw him, she was in pain because she wanted to be the one talking to him. It felt as though there was a divide between them because the adults and the younger teenagers were separated, and since it was her party, Rachel was locked in with the younger crowd. She continually fingered the pendant than hung around her neck. She was the envy of all the other girls, and it felt nice to have it resting against her skin. It was like she had a part of him around her neck, a symbol that she meant something to him. She couldn't imagine that he'd give something this beautiful to just anyone, and she began to convince herself that there was something more. After all, she was 18 now, she was a woman. He was a man. Sure, there may have been some social taboos, but they all had their desires. It wasn't as though there was anything criminal about it.

But making it a reality was something different entirely. It was all well and good having the fantasy, but Rachel had no idea how to take it further. She wished she could just march up to him and tell him how she felt, but if he refused, it would be humiliating and cause irreparable damage between Daniel, herself, and her parents. She hoped to get him alone at some point so they could talk

149

again, and she could gauge if there really was some attraction lingering between them, which was why she kept looking for him. However, her friends seemed determined to keep her to themselves.

At one point, she excused herself to go and get a drink. The tables of food and drink were outside by the pool, and most people had gravitated away from them so she was able to enjoy a few moments alone. Away from all these people, the air was cooler, and goosebumps prickled on her skin.

She poured herself a drink.

"You look great," someone said. It took her by surprise and she jumped, almost spilling the contents of the cup she was holding. Rachel turned around to see Mark standing there. He looked good in his suit, but it wasn't he Rachel wanted to talk to.

"Thank you," she said, and dipped her head, indicating that she was going to walk away, but Mark stepped to the side, blocking her exit. He reached out and put a hand on her arm. It was a light gesture and there was no malice behind it, but she still didn't like it.

"Where are you going? We've barely had a chance to speak tonight," he said earnestly.

"I know, but there are a lot of people here. I've never had such a fuss made over me before," Rachel said.

"You deserve to have a fuss made over you. At least we get a chance to have a little chat now. Are you having a good time?"

"I am."

"That's good. Listen, Rachel, I wanted to talk to you about something. We've known each other a while now and high school is coming to an end soon. There's going to be a point where a lot of us here probably aren't going to ever see each other again. I don't really like thinking about it myself, but it's just the way it is I suppose. Anyway, I don't want that to happen to us. It's just that…I've had feelings for you for a while now and I haven't known how to tell you, so I thought that I'd just come right out and say it. Rachel, will you go out with me?"

Rachel could hear the tension in his voice and could almost smell it exuding from his body. Part of her thought she should say yes. After all, he was a popular guy and she knew a number of girls who had crushes on him. It was normal for her to go out with someone her own age, but when she looked at Mark the only thing she thought was that he wasn't Daniel.

"I'm sorry, Mark, I just don't feel the same way. I really appreciate it thought, and you know Hannah and Amy both-"

"What do you mean you don't feel the same way? Why not?" he asked, glowering. A dark energy had taken hold of him, and she was suddenly aware how much bigger and stronger he was.

"Well…I just, you know, not everyone can like everyone else. I'm really flattered, but I think it's best if you ask someone else."

Mark almost vibrated with tension. A strange look came over his face, as though he didn't understand what was happening. His hands clenched into fists and he spoke in a low tone, clenching his jaw.

"Rachel, that isn't what you're supposed to say. Come on, just give me a chance and you'll see that I'm a good guy. This is your birthday. Something special is supposed to happen. Just give me a chance. Come on, let's go upstairs and have a chat. There's so much you don't know about me. That's probably why you're a little hesitant, but once you get to know me everything will be better," he said.

Rachel gulped. Fear had caused a lump to form in her throat.

"Mark, seriously, I think you might have had a bit too much to drink or something." At least, she hoped that was the excuse because otherwise he was showing a very dark side to him. Mark stepped forward, closing the distance between them even further, and fear began to spike inside her. She glanced over his shoulder to try and get the attention of anyone else, but it seemed as though they were miles away from the rest of the party. She stepped back, and he stepped with her.

"Mark, I think we should get back to the party now and forget that this ever happened."

"No, I'm not forgetting this. I really like you, Rachel, and I think we could be great together. Why don't you just go out with me one time? That's all I ask, then, if you still feel the same way, we can call it quits and there are no hard feelings. All it takes is one date, that's not so much to ask, is it?"

"I think the lady already made her feelings clear," Daniel said. Her heart leaped with relief when he emerged from the darkness. Mark scowled at him. She was worried that he was going to say something back or try and fight Daniel, but it seemed as though Daniel's forceful stare was enough to make him leave. Mark went off muttering to himself. She steadied herself against the table and breathed a sigh of relief.

"Are you okay?" Daniel asked, placing a reassuring hand on her shoulder. She nodded. Daniel looked back to make sure that Mark was leaving. "Unfortunately, some men don't know that no means no."

"I just don't get it. It's like over the past few months, everyone has been looking at me different."

"I guess it's different for girls than it is for boys. Suddenly, you became works of art, and all the men want to possess you, but very few of them understand how to make you feel valued and appreciated. Those boys have got a lot to learn. Hopefully, most of them will, and they won't make you or other girls uncomfortable again."

"It's all so messed up. Thank you for coming to my rescue."

"Anytime," Daniel said, smirking. His hand was still resting against her shoulder. She suddenly became very aware of his flesh against hers. All it would have taken was the slightest movement of his fingers and her strap could have been pulled away, falling down the top of her arm, exposing her skin even further.

Daniel took his hand away.

"Was it easy for you, growing up?"

Daniel barked a laugh. "Oh, hell no. I was the most awkward boy you'd ever meet. It took me longer than most to get to grips with life and figure out what I really wanted and who I was, but eventually I got there."

"I hope it doesn't take me as long as you."

"You seem to have a firm grip on what you want. Your parents did a good job raising you."

"I like to think so. Thank you for saying that. It's nice for someone to treat me like an adult."

"Well, you are an adult now. You're a beautiful young woman." She blushed when he said that.

"So, what is it you want?" she asked. Her voice trembled as she was trying to be flirtatious with him, but she didn't know if he was catching onto the signals she was giving him. She didn't even know if he would see her as a sexual being. Rachel feared that he had placed her in the category of 'friend's daughter, never to be touched.'

A strange look came over Daniel's face, and he pursed his lips. The corner of his mouth twitched into a smile.

"I think that's better left unspoken. I wouldn't want to corrupt you on your 18th birthday."

Rachel's heart skipped a beat as she thought about what could be corrupting about him.

"No, please, tell me."

Daniel looked tempted, she could tell, but something was still holding him back. He looked around, as if to make sure there was nobody else in earshot, and then let out a rush of breath.

"No, I don't think we're ready to have this conversation. Maybe you should go back to your friends and enjoy the rest of your party." He motioned to walk away, but Rachel wasn't having that.

"Don't do that," she said. The words came out more sternly than she had anticipated, but she wasn't going to apologize for them. Daniel arched an eyebrow at her.

"Excuse me?" he said, taken aback.

"Don't treat me like I'm a child. You've been calling me a woman all evening, so don't treat me like you know better than me. I'm 18 now. I can handle anything."

"You've certainly got some fire about you, Rachel," he said. He still seemed hesitant, but he hadn't moved away yet. "Okay, I apologize for treating you like a child. I didn't mean any disrespect. It's just that I have some…unique interests, and I don't think your parents would appreciate us having this conversation."

"As far as I can see, they're not here. This has nothing to do with them. You and I are just two people in this universe."

Daniel had a measuring gaze, and his eyes roamed over her body. Rachel held her head high determined to not show any sign of weakness. She was curious about what he had to say and wanted to prove to him that she could indeed handle this secret. She knew that this was her moment to transform herself before his eyes, to show him that she wasn't just a girl, that she was something more.

Daniel lowered his voice so that it was barely a whisper and moved closer to her, but not threateningly like Mark had. This was more intimate, cozier.

"Are you aware of BDSM?" he asked.

"You mean, like in Fifty Shades of Grey?" she replied. Rachel's mind was alive now. She'd heard a few things about it, but didn't know what it really entailed.

"It's a little like that, but the reality is a lot different. It's all about trust and communication between a submissive and a dominant."

"Okay…so the submissive just does whatever it takes to please a dominant?"

"Sometimes, but there's more to it than that. The submissive gives herself to the dominant and trusts that he will respect her limits and teach her how to feel pleasure. He guides her, owns her, trains her to fulfill their mutual desires. I believe that everyone in this world is either submissive or dominant. There's a core inside you that either craves power or craves to be dominated by it. It's the most exhilarating, wonderful release in the world, and I've never felt anything more intense than when I take a submissive to train, but it's not for everyone. It's an intoxicating thing, and once you take a step into the kinky world, you can never return to the vanilla life."

"What kind of things do you do?" Rachel asked, her voice almost catching in her throat. She would never have guessed that this could happen, but she found herself listening intently. When he mentioned the idea of submitting to a dominant, it had sparked something inside her, and she knew on which side of the spectrum she fell.

"Many things. It depends on the submissive, but I personally enjoy degradation, bondage, primal play-"

"I don't know what any of those mean. Why degradation? Isn't that mean?"

"A little, but sometimes a dominant has to be a little mean, especially if the submissive isn't being a good girl. But I see degradation as a form of endearment and affection."

"I'm still not sure I understand. Can you give me an example?"

"Well, it would be me saying that you're a cute teen slut, a young girl made to be trained into the perfect plaything for a younger man, ready to be used and abused and forced into her rightful place, an 18-year-old toy."

The moment he said those words, something rippled through Rachel's body, and she was in heaven. Nobody had ever spoken to her like that, but the power and confidence with which Daniel spoke was like a drug. He spoke to her in a way that seemed like he already owned her, and she wanted nothing more than to be his plaything.

"What's my rightful place?" she asked, her voice small and meek, but her heart beat with the fury of a dragon. Daniel was inches away from her now. His body bristled with erotic heat. The air sizzled between them.

"Where do you think it is?" he challenged.

"On the bed?" she asked innocently.

Daniel smirked. "Close, but it's on your knees with your hands in your lap and your mouth hanging open ready to service me."

Rachel was floored with the way he spoke. Suddenly, Daniel had turned from a charming gentleman into a confident man blazing with erotic heat. A new countenance had come over him, and she had never been more attracted to him. He went on to explain the other things he was interested in, and Rachel was hanging off every word. It all sounded so intense and wonderful, and it all felt *right*. He was talking to her about things she wanted deeply, things she had never known existed before this conversation, but she knew that she couldn't live without them. No wonder an ordinary relationship never appealed to her, not when this alternative was available.

"And how do I become yours? How do I become your 18-year-old slut?" she asked. When she spoke, it was as though it was somebody else speaking, and yet it was the truest thing she had ever said. It was as though by accepting this role as a submissive she was casting off years of falsehood and uncertainty. She was accepting her truth and stripping away the façade that had been built as a polite young woman.

"We should go inside. Sneak into your room," he said. The thought of sneaking around with him was so illicit. Rachel's eyes gleamed with hunger, and they quickly went into the room. Nobody would ever have suspected that he was taking her upstairs to teach her more about BDSM and the kink lifestyle, and none of them thought anything of the two of them spending time together, but in their hearts each of them knew that they had a taboo secret, and the thought of exploring it made Rachel's desire sing.

***

Rachel and Daniel went upstairs to her room, and the noises of the party faded away. Rachel was a little embarrassed about the stuffed animals on the bed, but Daniel told her not to worry; he thought it was cute. He sat her down on the bed and explained carefully and slowly about what being a submissive truly meant. He taught her about limits and encouraged her to ask questions so that she was properly informed. Rachel sat there dutifully with her hands in her lap, loving the way he explained everything and showed her exactly what this new world entailed. She smiled at him with excitement, and her mind bubbled with questions. When he mentioned rules, she was curious about what rules he had for the submissives he took under his guidance.

"I won't tell you all of them right now," he said, "but a few of them are that you're to end any message to me with a kiss to show me proper respect. You are to address me as Sir or Master. I would have you complete any tasks I set for you within a reasonable timeframe. I consider your body mine so I want you to flaunt it for me, making yourself my personal model, posing for me and surprising me with pictures. I would expect you to be honest with me at all times and make sure that you tell me whenever you feel uncomfortable. I will also take control of what you wear and choose your outfits. Everything you do is in service of your submission to me."

Rachel looked up at him with wide eyes. He spoke with such authority, with such command.

"I want to be yours, Master. I want to be your little teenage slut," she said. The words felt so natural coming from her. She could already feel herself submitting to him in her mind. She looked up at his towering body, his masculine physique, and she knew that she wanted to be owned by him, and she desperately hoped that he would take her.

He came up to her and cupped his hand under her chin, tilting her head up.

"You have the prettiest eyes," he said. "Now get on your knees."

Rachel did as she was told. She crawled off the bed and sank to her knees. The pendant hung off her neck. She placed her hands in her lap, just as he wanted, and continued to look up at him. Daniel held out his hand. She placed hers in his. Her hand looked tiny in his. She was so small, petite, especially when she was below him like this, but she knew it was where she belonged.

"Do you, Rachel, consent to be my submissive, my teenage slut, to offer your body to me and vow to offer your obedience?"

"I do," she said eagerly.

"Then I hereby claim you as my submissive. I take you as my 18-year-old slut. You're now owned by an older man, how do you feel?"

"Wonderful. Happy. But what do we do now?" Rachel asked.

"Now, your training begins," he said.

***

Rachel was helped up and out of her dress. Daniel reached behind her and pulled the long zipper down, and the dress fell away, exposing her naked body. At first, Rachel felt vulnerable because she had never been on display like this before, but Daniel pulled her arms away to properly expose her and murmured his delight at her body. He placed his hand on her hips and turned her around, making sure that he got a good look. As the moments passed, she found that she liked being on display for him.

"You look good enough to use," he breathed into her ear. Rachel's body tingled. Her breaths were short and sharp in anticipation of what Daniel was going to do. Anything might happen, and it was more exciting than even when she had been to Disneyworld.

His hands looked so large and strong against her milky pure skin. He wrapped them around her waist and pulled her into him. She felt the heat of his body and the swelling arousal in his crotch. His hands roamed around her shoulders, always teasing her because she wanted him to touch the areas that were burning with desire. His fingers ran through her hair, and his hand curled around her neck, squeezing tightly, and Rachel felt her knees weakening. Her body was his, and she let him touch anywhere he wanted. His hands moved down to cup her breasts, squeezing the soft flesh and stroking the hard nipples. Rachel closed her eyes as her body burst with all kinds of sensations. Her mind grew hazy as his hands reached down and stroked the burning insides of her thigh. She cringed, for nobody else had ever touched her there before, but his fingers were ardent and he seemed satisfied to feel the wet heat between her legs.

"On your knees again," he said.

As she descended to the floor without hesitation, he pulled his tie away and unbuttoned his shirt, revealing his sculpted physique. Rachel gazed at him with intense desire.

"Undo my belt," he ordered. Rachel reached up with trembling hands and undid the clasp. Daniel stepped out of his pants, and Rachel gazed at the huge bulge swelling inside. He took the belt from her hands and wrapped it around her neck, tightening it like a collar.

"For now this will have to do, but I'll get you a proper collar to go around your neck. Your neck should never be bare," he said. Then, he took her hands and brought them to his waist and used them to peel away his underwear. She watched as his thick, long erection spilled out of his boxers and her mouth hung open in awe.

"Oh my God," she gasped, but she barely had time to say anything because Daniel grabbed a fistful of her hair and brought her head forward, smearing her with the heat of his sex. She opened her mouth wide and caught his erection in her mouth and began sucking on it deeply. Daniel had a firm hold of her head, and an intense energy seemed to come over him. He had a tight grip on her and used this to take control of her head, pushing her back and forth, so that all she had to do was sit there and let him use her mouth. She looked up at him and felt the heat from his erection fill her mouth. Her eyes began to water, but she kept her mouth open, wanting to take him deeper and deeper inside.

The feeling of submission ran rampant through her body and gave her a release that was akin to finding her purpose in life. The clarity was astounding. When she was on her knees, she knew her place, and when she was pleasuring her master, she knew what she was put on this world to do. She loved hearing him moan and groan and grunt. His older body tensed, and his muscles were taut. He was so strong, and eventually he seemed to have enough of using her mouth.

"We're going to have to be quiet. Can't have anyone discovering us in here. This has to be our little secret," he said, dragging her up by the belt and shoving her onto the bed. She landed with a thud, and he was on top of her instantly. Daniel used his strength to pin her down, taking her slender wrists into one hand and putting them above her head. His other hand trailed down her breasts and then dug into her inner thighs, before traveling up to the shaved delta in between her legs. Rachel groaned. Her body arched. His fingers found the hot wetness, and she trembled as he thrust his fingers inside her. They danced wildly, and she shuddered and writhed, loving how she struggled to escape without any hope. Her body felt as though it was on fire, and his hot breath washed over her skin. Her mind cracked at the intense pleasure. His fingers reached inside her so deeply that she was sure they were touching her soul.

He leaned down to kiss and bite her neck and breasts, taking her nipples in between his teeth. Rachel began to moan. She tried to be quiet, but the pleasure was just too intense. There was nothing she could do to stop herself. It all just felt too good.

Daniel stopped and glared at her.

"I told you we had to be quiet," he said.

"I'm so sorry, Sir. I just can't help it. You're making me feel so good."

"We can't have this," he said, and picked up the tie that he had thrown on the floor. He shoved it in her mouth, gagging her, silencing her, and then resumed playing with her. Now Rachel's moans were muffled. Daniel held her head down, pushing it to the side as he plunged his fingers inside her. She thrummed with desire and lust as he forced the orgasm from her, playing with her so intensely, so savagely, that it produced the most erotic pleasure she had ever felt. It built inside her and swelled dramatically and then suddenly there was a super nova inside and her entire body exploded with heat, but Daniel didn't stop there. He kept going, making her wet again. His hand was already drenched and she could feel the slickness seep over her thighs. She tried to beg for him to stop, but her words were muffled by the gag. The pleasure came sweeping over her again and again, relentlessly, and there was no resistance she could possibly offer to calm her soul.

Her body was flushed and drained. Her mind had cracked. When Daniel finally extricated his fingers from her body, she had lost count of how many times she had climaxed. They all blurred into one another and her mind was drained, but Daniel wasn't finished with her. She looked at him through bleary eyes and saw how his fingers glistened with her juice. He adjusted his position so that he was directly over her and placed his hand on her neck, choking her, holding her down. His eyes were wild, and she could see he had given into some primal energy. She opened her mouth as widely as she could, feeling in danger, yet also knowing that he would take care of her.

He pushed apart her legs and slid into her effortlessly. Rachel groaned as she felt his experienced older erection thrust into her virgin teenage body. He fucked her without mercy, moving his hips like a machine, grunting and pressing his head against hers. She felt the sweat from his forehead and breathed in the sexy scent of his hot body as he dominated her. Her whole world became him, and she could feel herself giving into him mind, body, and soul. He owned every part of her, and it was the most delirious feeling she had ever enjoyed. She was taken to another realm, and the submission she felt was magical.

Daniel made love to her, fucked her, cherished her, used her. She was his submissive, his teen slut, his virgin, and his lover. He spanked her breasts and made her suck on his fingers and completely owned her body. When he came, it was with a shuddering earthquake, and a feeling of thunder and lightning crashing through her body.

They lay there, panting, dripping with sweat. Daniel leaned down to kiss her lightly, and he stroked her hair. He took his hands away and undid the belt. He pulled her close and held her tightly. The rush of emotion almost made her want to cry. There were still so many things she didn't understand, but she was confident that he would teach her all she needed to know.

"There's just one more thing," he said, and went to her desk to pull out a pen. He wrote MLS on the inside of her left wrist. "This is a reminder that you are owned by me. Look at it any time you need to feel happy. If anyone asks you, just tell them it's there to remind you of something."

Rachel smiled at him and kissed him lovingly. She was his, completely and utterly, and she had never felt happier.

About Alexandra Noir

Alexandra Noir is a social worker. She's always had dirty fantasies locked inside of her mind and now loves writing about them and occasionally experiencing them. Her free time often consists of BDSM play where she submits to men that can bring her to places most women only dream of. Every so often though, she finds herself on the other side of the flogger and can bring a man to his knees.

She writes about BDSM, kink, and power exchange. You can join her email list here and get a free story! You'll also hear about how to get my books as soon as they come out and be able to pre-order them for just 99 cents.